RIDING FOR CUSTER

TOM CURRY

WHEELER
CHIVERS

This Large Print edition is published by Wheeler Publishing, Waterville, Maine, USA and by BBC Audiobooks Ltd, Bath, England.
Wheeler Publishing, a part of Gale, Cengage Learning.
Copyright © 1947 by Tom Curry.
Copyright © renewed 1975 by Tom Curry.
The moral right of the author has been asserted.

ALL RIGHTS RESERVED
The text of this Large Print edition is unabridged.
Other aspects of the book may vary from the original edition.
Set in 16 pt. Plantin.

LIBRARY OF CONGRESS CATALOGING-IN-PUBLICATION DATA

Curry, Tom, 1900–
  Riding for Custer / by Tom Curry.
    p. cm. — (Wheeler Publishing large print western)
  ISBN-13: 978-1-4104-2606-2 (pbk. : alk. paper)
  ISBN-10: 1-4104-2606-8 (pbk. : alk. paper)
  1. Large type books. I. Title.
PS3505.U9725R53 2010
813'.52—dc22   2010004446

BRITISH LIBRARY CATALOGUING-IN-PUBLICATION DATA AVAILABLE

Published in 2010 in the U.S. by arrangement with Golden West Literary Agency.
Published in 2010 in the U.K. by arrangement with Golden West Literary Agency.

U.K. Hardcover: 978 1 408 49112 6 (Chivers Large Print)
U.K. Softcover: 978 1 408 49113 3 (Camden Large Print)

Printed in the United States of America
1 2 3 4 5 6 7 14 13 12 11 10

RIDING FOR CUSTER

CHAPTER I
REIGN OF BLOOD

Up from the Indian Territory, set off by the United States Government for the use of the savage tribes, rode the red horde, crossing into southern Kansas where the scattered settlements and ranches, the lonely sodhouse farmers, slept with one eye open and bated breath, fearful of the lithe and murderous killers.

Bands of roving Indians were to be feared at all times, but especially in the full of the moon when, on their wiry, hairy mustangs, they raided for hundreds of miles. Stock was never safe unless strongly guarded and, worse, women and children were in greater danger than from death and the scalping knife. The savages carried them off as hostages, for use as slaves.

The large band, on the blanketed backs of their small, swift horses, were painted for the warpath. Eagle feathers bobbed black against the silver night sky, as the redman band splashed across the stony creek ford and on to the rolling plains.

From their tribal markings, these Indians were Cheyennes and Kiowas, blood allies, two hard-fighting nations led by ruthless and devilishly clever chieftains.

In the van rode the Three. On the left, mounting a beautiful, long-limbed silver gray which melted into the moonlight like a ghost, was a giant Kiowa with a broad, high-boned face, wide, thin-lipped, cruelly twisted mouth, black, piercing eyes, and the curved nose of his kind. His black hair hung straight and shoulder long, brushing the golden epaulets of the major-general's tunic he sported. On his breast hung a medallion, to him a magic and protective charm.

"Satanta," growled the big man riding next to the giant, "tonight I will show Black Kettle and you I am your blood-brother." The whites of the speaker's eyes contrasted oddly against the black of his skin, but he spoke in the Cheyenne tongue.

He wore fringed deerskin breeches, beaded moccasins, streaks of yellow war-paint curved down his grim, ebony-hued cheeks. The cool autumn wind was staved off by a leather shirt, and in his hair stood an eagle feather.

He was answered by the third man of the

trio — Black Kettle, the great Cheyenne chief who had succeeded Roman Nose, the Butcher, when the latter died in battle.

"Black Buffalo," the chief grunted, "you have been our friend. These new guns are good, better than the white soldiers have. We will never surrender to our enemies. Both Satanta and I swear it. And we know that though the hated blood of the white man runs in your veins, yet your heart is Indian."

Black Buffalo patted the fine sporting rifle under his burly leg.

"Tonight this shall speak for the Indian, Black Kettle," he promised. "Yes, you will find the rifles carry farther and stronger than the soldier carbines of Yellow Hair. You must thank me for them."

"We do," replied Satanta, stolidly. "At first Moketavata and I believed it was the yellow metal which caused Father Vandon to give us these new guns so secretly. But now we see it was you."

Black Buffalo understood the Kiowa's veiled sarcasm. He was silent for a moment, then said earnestly:

"Satanta, it's true that white men put great store in the yellow metal. But it was I who made Vandon get the guns for you."

"Ugh," grunted Black Kettle, his keen

black eyes on the dark shapes of several buildings ahead, set on the bank of a small stream. "The time has come. Satanta, do you and your braves drive off the horses while Black Buffalo and I will take care of the men who rush out."

Circling silently, the lithe red men under Black Kettle and the man who sought their trust, dismounted and crept in upon the dark, sleeping settlement. Some two hundred armed Cheyennes, painted hideously for the kill, got in on the half dozen pitiful little shacks, built from sod bricks and the scant timber cut from the belt along the Kansas creek. Horses and cattle grazed in a great common corral, and Satanta rode with his Kiowas to run these off.

Black Kettle gave the signal, an ear-piercing, blood-curdling shriek that sent the chill of death to the heart of the whites awakened by it.

Red brands flared, were tossed to the thatched roofs of huts or barns. Through the settlement rushed the fierce attackers.

Gunshots banged from the narrow windows. A red glow rose high into the night sky, blotting out the moon with smoke and crimson light. Flitting, elusive, merciless devils shot into the windows, whooping their hate.

Black Buffalo, seeking to show his good will toward the Indians, dashed to the largest shack, crept along the wall with a six-shooter in one hand. A settler was banging steadily away with a large-caliber Sharps buffalo gun. Black Buffalo waited until the white man showed for an instant to take aim. With a wild shriek, Black Buffalo bobbed up and shot him through the brain.

A woman shrieked inside. A child began to cry: "Daddy — Daddy!"

Black Buffalo, grinning evilly, picked up a burning torch and flung it into the smoke-filled cabin. He found a heavy chunk of rail, and, with the other Indians shrieking and shooting, he beat in the door of the house.

Cheyennes raced up as he rushed inside. A bullet, sent by the brave wife of the settler, cut a piece of flesh from his arm, but then he was upon her, crushing her to the earthen floor. His tomahawk flashed.

The screams of tortured victims melted into the general confusion. Wounded men were driven out, and arrows were shot into them until they seemed feathered with the missiles. Bullets were too valuable to be wasted if it could be helped.

The horror of the Indian massacre swirled on in bloody death.

Screaming women, seeking in vain to hold

their babies and shield the older children from the fiercely bedaubed red murderers, were struck vicious tomahawk blows or driven to the ground by rifle stocks. These people of the south Kansas Frontier, hard-working, home-loving folks, were victims of a terror beyond human description.

A giant Dog Soldier, whose eagle-feather headdress swept the ground, and whose broad red face was smeared with black, yellow and pink patterns of color, beat down a sturdy settler with his hatchet, literally hacking him to pieces. Another ferocious warrior, also a member of the evil Dog Soldiers, a band formed of all the worst elements among the various tribes, drove a feathered arrow into another Kansan at close range.

As the settler fell, the brave touched him with his coup stick. Only a scalp taken in battle in this way counted toward a warrior's credits. His long-bladed scalping-knife flashed in the rising ruby light from the burning houses. Hanging the scalp in his belt, the Dog Soldier again joined the other whooping, leaping devils.

Everywhere in the little settlement similar scenes were being enacted. Then the wails began dying off as victim after victim perished or lost consciousness. The massacre had reached its insane peak, then began descending when only pitifully still figures lay, dead and dying, in the blazing ruins of the homes.

Hysterical young wives of murdered settlers were tied up and slung over mustangs, to be carried to the hidden Indian villages. They would be slaves to the squaws and their life among the savages an unbelievable nightmare. Several children who had not been killed, might be adopted into the tribes as Indians.

Leaving behind them the blazing settlement and the still bodies that so short a time before had been warm-blooded, living men and women with all the love and hope and cares of such, the Dog Soldiers started back for Indian Territory, chanting a paean of savage triumph.

At Black Buffalo's belt hung the long-tressed scalp of a woman, the shorter-haired topknot of a man.

"Have I not proved I am all Indian tonight?" he demanded of Satanta and Black Kettle.

"Ugh," grunted Black Kettle, staring straight ahead.

"You have done well, Black Buffalo," Satanta said. "And yet, how can we be sure you will forget forever the white blood that flows in your veins? The Indian must guard well his secrets from his sworn foe, the *wa-sichu.*"

"But with the yellow metal we can defeat the *wasichu,* the white devil! You and Black Kettle need me, Satanta. I know the plans of the whites. Sheridan even now plans to strike the Dog Soldiers, the Cheyennes and Kiowas! He has sent Custer — Pahuska, Long Hair — to Fort Dodge to deal with you. And his new Seventh Cavalry is pinin' for action."

Satanta patted the golden epaulets of his major-general's uniform.

"Long Hair, Yellow Hair, Custer!" he boasted. "What does Satanta care for him? He is a fool. He gave me this, and many other presents, just because I made promises to him! Promises I never meant to keep. I don't fear Long Hair."

"Maybe you fooled Custer once," growled Black Buffalo, "but you won't again, Satanta. He's learned a lot against the Sioux." He drew the back of his hand across his throat, sign language symbol for the mighty Sioux, who always cut their victim's throat.

"The Sioux are the friends of the Cheyennes," Black Kettle said.

"You need spies in the white men's camps, I tell you," insisted Black Buffalo. "And information only I can get for you."

Satanta looked at Black Kettle who shrugged, grunted. Satanta pointed toward the western line of the Nation.

"The hills," he said to Black Buffalo.

"The Antelope Hills?"

"Ugh," grunted Satanta, then added: "We need more bullets for these new guns, Black Buffalo."

"You shall have them! Where — in the Antelopes?"

But he could worm nothing more from them about their secret hiding place. Maddeningly he had been checked by the devious processes of the Indian mind.

The trading post, one of the branches of the Indian Affairs Commission, stood on the lower Cimarron River in the Nation, the territory assigned to many savage tribes as a reservation to keep them from slaying and raiding the white settlers of the States.

The store was of unbarked wood, and the agent's house was a square structure with a wide veranda. Across the river, on the flat, stood many Indian tepees. The red wards of the Government had come to draw clothing and rations to trade their furs and gold and other treasures.

It was night and lamplight shone from the agent's windows as an Indian rode up, dismounted, and stepped to the porch. He pushed in the door without knocking and entered.

It was the ferocious Black Buffalo, with dirt and dried gore on his deerskin garments.

The Indian agent, John Vandon, a big man with a long, shaggy, unkempt mane, a bristling black beard and deep-set, piggish green eyes, cursed and swung in his chair to see who had entered so unceremoniously.

"So it's you, Henderson," he said in his deep bass growl.

Vandon was a man of positive character, as exemplified by his sun-cured hide, his heavy snout and great, hairy hands. But behind his rugged, powerful exterior was a grasping nature that would do anything for profit.

A killer by profession, he had bribed his way to this lucrative spot. He had no desire to help his unfortunate red wards. His only motive in running the agency was to feather his own nest by stealing from the Government and by cheating the Indians of their furs and valuables.

Black Buffalo, whom Vandon had called Henderson, threw himself into a chair and reached for the whiskey bottle. In his eyes was a wolfish ferocity that showed there was no mercy in him. But so powerful was this criminal that even the giant Vandon feared him and catered to him.

A third man in the room was a member of this brutal trio which sought to dominate the Indian Nation and Kansas.

He was a tall fellow with a long, horse face and stiff, dry tow hair that stuck straight up. His beard and mustache were so light that they scarcely showed against his reddish skin.

"Hello, Chief," he said to Henderson, deep respect for this super-criminal in his voice.

"Glad to see you, Horseface," rumbled the man who rode as Black Buffalo.

"Horseface" Keyes pulled up a box close to Henderson. He wore a soldier's blue coat and military trousers shoved into Army boots. He was a veteran of the Civil War in which he had distinguished himself by shirking all hard labor and in evading any dangers of the battlefield. Now, on the Frontier, he was a fit aide to such a man as Vandon, a henchman who would commit any crime on order. His only motive was to get his hands on as much money as he could, any way at all.

"How'd yuh make out, Chief?" he asked eagerly.

Black Buffalo cursed. "The old goats tried to put me off again, boys! Three nights ago we struck Pepperville, Kansas, and wiped it out. I did my best to talk over Satanta and Black Kettle, but all they did let slip was that they get their gold in the Antelope Hills!"

"The Antelopes, huh!" Vandon exclaimed excitedly. "Where? The Antelopes are purty big."

"They wouldn't tell me."

Vandon's excitement crashed. "Aw, they never will tell a white man where they find it, Boss. They've been bringin' nuggets for a year but never say where they dig 'em from. I've tried likker and everything else."

Black Buffalo laughed. He reached inside his deerskin jacket, drew forth a little hide pouch. From this he spilled onto the table several chunks of rock, and the lamplight caught the scintillating golden veins thick in the ore.

Agent Vandon gasped. "Yuh got it!"

"I believe so. I shook Satanta and Black Kettle and rode over to the Antelopes yesterday. It didn't take me long to find these, in Sand Creek that runs into the Canadian." He scooped up the nuggets, returned them to their sack. "We've got to keep it quiet, boys. And we've got to figure how to get it out for ourselves. The Indians'll never let us mine there, that's a cinch. Besides, right now, Satanta and Black Kettle think they can lick the whole U.S. Army. The fools! I'll get even with the red rascals for lyin' to me."

"Just the same," Horseface Keyes objected, "we can't do much while the Indians're so strong, Boss. So what good is the gold yuh've found?"

"We've got to look at it the long way," replied the disguised man. "The Indians can't hold on to that north strip for long. There's already talk of another state being made of it. The worse the Indians behave, the quicker they'll be crushed. Satanta and Black Kettle will attack the Kansas settlements wholesale with a little encouragement, hit 'em hard. I'll see to that. In the meantime we make plenty furnishin' 'em guns and ammunition — likker, too, no matter if it is forbidden. They bring in their furs and gold to you, Vandon, and we make a thousand percent profit — plenty to run on, to pay your boys here. In the long run there'll be a railroad through southern Kansas, openin' up the Territory, and straight to our mines. We'll own that line."

"How?" challenged Vandon. "Kansas is homesteaded, ain't it?"

The streaked, blacked face set in cruel lines.

"It won't be when Satanta and Black Kettle get through — under my direction!"

CHAPTER II
ARMY SCOUTS

"Tie a cloth round that fool mule's muzzle, Joe. One song'll fetch that whole passel of red devils on us."

The speaker, a handsome young man, keen of feature, and with a reckless air, replaced the field glasses to his blue eyes, regarding the war party of savages filing along the band of timber fringing the southern Kansas creek.

"Shucks," murmured "California Joe," to whom he had spoken. "Mabel don't sing 'less she's requested, Rio Kid. Look, yuh've hurt her feelin's. Why, she knowed them pesky Kiowas was over there 'fore we did! She ain't hankerin' to be took prisoner and hafta work for the squaws."

"Yuh've got sharp eyes, Joe. They are Kiowas. Sprinklin' of Cheyennes with 'em."

"Uh-huh. All workin' together, Kid. They ain't been as bold as this since the Civil War kept everybody too busy to fight 'em.

Cheyennes, Kiowas, Arapahoes, Comanches, Sioux, even Apaches are ridin' the trails up here. That there Nation they been given is home base for 'em, that's all."

Bob Pryor, the Rio Kid, not so long ago, Captain Robert Pryor of the U.S. Army and Custer's Brigade, passed the glasses to a tall, slim Mexican youth, in red sash and soft, form-fitting velvet garb, who squatted near him.

Through four terrible years of the Civil War, the Kid had fought for the Union, the right side as he saw it, though he had been born in Texas, on the Rio Grande. Captain Pryor then, he had been General George A. Custer's best aide-de-camp and scout.

But war had left a mark on him. His eyes now were devil-may-care, though shot with indomitable courage. His cheeks, bronzed by an outdoor life — for after the War he had never settled down, but had ridden the Western trails in search of excitement — glowed with youth and health. Under his cavalry Stetson, cocked and held by its strap at a rakish angle, his crisp chestnut hair was cropped short. His shoulders were broad, his waist narrow, and his was an ideal weight and size for a cavalryman, which he had been.

Mustered out after the War, he had remained a soldier at heart, but now he was on his own, fighting the evil elements of the great Frontier. An almost single-handed campaign, undertaken for the excitement it offered, and because he enjoyed the peril.

He was a fine figure of a man in his blue breeches with the faded yellow stripe down the seams, and tucked into short-spurred Army riding boots. A blue shirt, open at the V, gave a glimpse of the powerful chest. A wide black leather belt gripped his waist, supporting holsters for his two Army Colts. Slung across his shoulders was a cartridge belt of ammunition for his small arms. More bullets were in his pockets, and under his shirt were a couple of extra, hidden revolvers.

Four years as a cavalryman had made him a deadly shot from horseback. And Saber, the Kid's mount that to him was almost human — the mouse-colored dun with the black stripe down his ridgy backbone, "the breed that never dies" — was trained to aid his rider at such deadly work.

Danger was a tonic to this man. For so many years had death been close to his heels, that to expect it was familiar to him. Yet, though careless of life, he was not so about his own appearance. Through army training and a natural bent he had a passion for neatness, and never neglected his gear or himself.

Celestino Mireles, the Kid's comrade of the Danger Trail, was a tall, hawk-faced Mexican youth, with the fighting blood of proud hidalgos flowing in his veins. His deep-set eyes, curved nose, and full lips showed his patrician descent from the Conquistadores of Old Spain.

Mireles followed the Rio Kid with a blind devotion. To the young Mexican, whom the Kid had snatched from a cruel death at the Mireles *hacienda* in Mexico, the Rio Kid would always be "My General." Now, as from the wooded hilltop they regarded the band of marauding Indians, Mireles had tied a bandanna around the muzzle of his handsome coffee-colored mare, whose mane was several shades lighter than her hide. Mabel, California Joe's mule, twitched her long ears, blinking her brown eyes.

"See?" whispered Joe. "That means her feelin's *are* hurt, Kid."

Pryor grinned. "Sorry, Mabel," he told the mule.

California Joe was a striking contrast to his two companions. He had long, flowing hair, a shaggy beard, a strong nose, and eyes a light but sharp blue. He was tall, and thin as a rail, but he was wearing so many layers of cu░░░░against the tang in the autumn air that he appeared bulky. Under the faded Army blue overcoat was a fringed buckskin jacket, pockets crammed with knicknacks — tobacco he so dearly loved, a bottle of whiskey, knives, string and hardtack. Under the overcoat was a deerskin windbreaker, then a vest, and a couple of ragged outer shirts, to say nothing of red flannel underwear.

One cheek was rounded out by his tobacco cud, seaming his sun-wrinkled eyes. The flat-brimmed black hat he wore had been discarded by someone else before he had acquired it, as had been most of his clothing. He wore moccasins instead of boots, since they were far more comfortable on his feet.

Despite his scarecrow getup, California Joe was the best known and most expert Indian scout available to the United States Army. So far, none of the generals had had any real experience fighting Indians, for they had been entirely engaged in the Civil War. Now it was over, they must learn new tricks of battle, the savage's way, in order to overcome the menace to the white man's westward expansion.

While these three watching men had their eyes trained on the redmen not so far in the distance, Saber, the Rio Kid's *dun* stood quietly, save for the light, sharp breathings and nervous twitchings which a white man's mount usually betrayed when it smelled Indians. Trained to a T, the dun merely rolled his eyes, one of which was merled, like a brown marble, streaked with white and blue. He was not muzzled, for he had been given warning to keep quiet — which was sufficient for Saber.

"General," Mireles said in a sudden whisper, "the Indians — zey see somezing!"

The Kid nodded, but did not answer. He shivered as a cold blast from the north hit him, stepped to Saber and unrolled a warm, fleece-lined leather jacket which he donned. Mireles, too, used to the warm skies of Mexico, was blue about the lips. He had wrapped an army overcoat about his slim form.

Watching the band of raiders, who were painted for the warpath, with feathers in their banded hair, and armed with latest repeating breech-loaders, the Kid and California Joe saw that Mireles was right. The Indians had sighted something, over the bulge of the rolling low hills, and were excited.

One of their scouts had come dashing back, flogging his hairy mustang, signaling with his raised arms. Instantly the band prepared for action. The Kid trained the field-glasses on the leaders.

"I believe that's Satanta up ahead, Joe, in that major-general's coat."

"Shore it's Satanta," agreed California Joe. "He's second head chief of the Kiowas, Kid. That's the uniform he wangled outa the Gen'ral." Joe grinned. "Gen'ral'll never forgive him for makin' a monkey outa him on that. 'Twas one of Custer's first dealin's with the Injuns."

"Who's that black-faced devil ridin' with Satanta?"

"Looks like a buffalo soldier, don't he? Mebbe a deserter from the army. Plenty of 'em around. He's painted like a Kiowa, but he don't ride just exactly like one of 'em."

For a time the Kid kept his glasses trained on the strange figure beside Satanta, whose golden epaulets caught the glint of the sunlight. By the aid of the magnifying glasses, which he carefully shielded from any chance sun ray that might flash a betrayal to the enemy, he could make out the curving yellow streaks on the black countenance of the other chief. But he could make out little else, for the man was wearing a thick blanket for warmth, and though feathers stuck up from his head, it

27

was partially covered by a coonskin hat.

The whole band — about seventy warriors — suddenly picked up speed, flying full-tilt along the creek and dropping out of sight of the spying Army scouts, sent into the Nation by Generals Sheridan and Custer, who were planning something here. For Fort Dodge was a hundred miles to the north, too far for the troops to strike at the elusive red raiders who had instituted a reign of blood on the Frontier.

There was no solution to the problem of the red men, whose life required huge areas of wilderness in which to hunt the game upon which he lived. Right or wrong, the progress of civilization demanded the death of the fabulous buffalo herds, the taming of the Frontier, railroads, and safety for women and children.

Pushed west, and then into ever decreasing reservations, it was not strange that the Indians fought desperately for survival. They fought in the only way they knew — savagely. But though they were barbarians, the cunning of the white man's brain outdid them at every turn.

The three scouts, preparing to mount and leave the vicinity, for they had no desire to tangle with such a formidable war party, heard the shooting as it roared on the crisp fall air. With the crack of rifles came the war-whoops of the savages.

"They got somebody," growled California Joe, but he could see nothing because of the intervening hillside.

Bung — bung — bung!

That was the reply to the first volley of the Kiowas' breech-loaders.

"Spencer carbines," the Kid said.

The rank-and-file of the U.S. Cavalry carried short-barreled Spencers. But they had nothing like the range of the rifles which Satanta and his braves sported.

Snap — snap!

"By golly, somebody's firin' a Colt at 'em, too!" exclaimed Joe.

"We better work down around that next break," ordered Pryor, stepping to Saber. "If yuh ask me, it's an army patrol, with an officer." The soldiers would be firing their Spencers, the officer his revolver.

It took them half an hour to work stealthily down the bank of the Kansas creek. Dismounting, they peered through the brakes across the stream at the battle hotly raging in a shallow depression.

Hard-riding, magnificent in their savagery, Indian braves swept a circle about a huddled blue-clad group, sheltered inside the crumbled walls of an adobe farmhouse.

Outside lay the dead cavalry horses, shot down in the first volleys from the Indians, to cut off flight for the troopers. In any case, the cavalry plugs would have stood no chance of outrunning the swift Plains mustangs.

"How'd that squad get down this far?" the Kid muttered, gripping his expensive, long-range rifle. He had unsheathed it from its saddle sling and carried it with him.

Plainly enough, this blackened farmhouse had been the scene of a recent Indian outrage, perhaps of the night before. For the ruins of the big barn still sent a column of smoke to the clear blue afternoon sky, mingling with the dust from the beating hoofs and the acrid powder vapor from exploded guns.

The Indians were attacking in their favorite, spectacular fashion. Each brave hung by a heel and one hand, on the far side of his mustang as he rode, exposing but a foot and a glimpse of head and shoulder for a target as he fired under or over the neck of his mount. The entire band of seventy were pouring bullets in at the troopers.

Through the drifting smoke and dust, the Rio Kid glimpsed an officer in cavalry Stetson and blue tunic, with the insignia of a lieutenant on his shoulder. He stood coolly up over his men, banging away at the attackers with an Army revolver.

"Young fool!" muttered Pryor, as he worked the mechanism, throwing a fresh shell into the firing-chamber of his rifle. "It's Lieutenant Dixon!"

CHAPTER III
ESCAPE

Pryor had met Lieutenant Frank Dixon, among many other Army officers, at the camp thirty miles southeast of Fort Dodge, Kansas, from which California Joe and he had started their scout.

A recruit fresh from West Point to the Seventh Cavalry, Dixon had had no battle experience and understood nothing of Indian warfare. He was, however, brave and altogether fearless, and the Kid had liked him from his first meeting with the youthful officer. The Kid had told himself then that young Dixon would learn in time — if given the time.

As he looked now, Dixon was whipped around as by an invisible hand, and suddenly popped down out of sight.

"Hit!" exclaimed the Kid.

But after a second, Dixon appeared again, this time shooting with his left hand, his right arm limp at his side.

"Well?" growled California Joe. "What're we waitin' for, Kid?"

"Let's go, boys!" the Kid said grimly. "Make as much racket and shoot fast as yuh can — and keep movin' if yuh value yore hide! Now!"

Satanta and the black-faced chief were over on the far side from them. Two troopers who had been hit lay quiet near the sod walls — dead, or their comrades would have brought them in.

Mireles, California Joe and Pryor took aim, and their rifles roared. Three Kiowas, fully exposed to them from their hidden position across the river, and intent on their prey in the center of the wide-flung circle, dropped dead from their horses at the accurate fire of the scouts.

"Again!" the Kid ordered in a ringing voice.

The never-failing marksmen picked targets, pulled trigger. Two more Indians received deadly lead, fell to the ground, their riderless mustangs dashing on. A third's horse slewed sideward and crashed head over heels, his Indian master flung through the air for thirty feet.

"I'll get him when he tries to mount," muttered Pryor.

And as the brave came up running, and

sought to hop a ride behind a comrade, the Kid's bullet got him in mid-air.

The smoke and roaring of their rifles told the attacking marauders of their position. Half the circling savages pulled around to shout and point at the veil of brush from behind which the busy trio were firing.

"Keep movin', boys!" warned the Kid. "If they savvy there's only three of us here, we're dead men!"

The savages had already formed to charge them, and were sweeping toward the low bank, opposite Pryor and his mates. Luckily the late Kansas homesteader had cleared the bush on his side of the stream, so that the Indians had no cover.

In a semi-crouch, the Rio Kid pulled trigger. The instant he had made his shot, he leaped to another position, whooping shrilly, and letting go once more as he landed. Each of his slugs hit either an Indian or a mustang, and he kept repeating his tactics of moving from spot to spot to make the enemy believe there were a dozen or more whites in the brush.

California Joe and Mireles were imitating the Kid. They made enough noise for a dozen men while their busy guns blared from fifty different spots.

The momentum of the Indians carried

them to the water, the horses sliding down the muddy bank, hock-deep in the creek. Pryor's rifle belched slugs into the fierce warriors, cutting their line, picking off sub-chiefs whom he could identify by their markings and feathers.

These seconds were moments of life or death. It was gun to gun, and bullets hailed through the screen of bush about the Kid and his companions.

A slug burned Pryor's ribs but did not stop him. He picked off a savage with yellow-and-purple daubs on his wide, rage-twisted face, a chief who had reached a point only feet from the Kid. Joe got two on the left flank, pressing in, and Celestino had the right.

"We got to convince 'em!" the Kid thought. If the whole gang charged the bank, some would get past, enough to finish them.

His guns blasted red-hot, faster and more furiously, in his expert hands, roaring defiance at the red enemy across the creek. Firing, leaping to a new point, shooting again, the three fighting scouts sought to convince the Indians that there were many attackers in ambush.

The ruse finally worked. The thirty Kiowas charging the creek at them lost twelve braves before they were halfway across. The survivors suddenly whipped their mustangs around and splashed for the north bank, urged on by the bullets from the grim-faced Kid and his aides.

Half of the original thirty made it, shrieking warnings to Satanta and the rest of the savages. It was not Indian strategy or nature to stand against odds. This was not considered clever. The heavy guns of the Rio Kid had convinced them they were being outflanked by a good-sized party, and without further hesitation, Satanta and the black-faced chief turned their mustangs and led the retreat. Within a minute, no Indians were in sight save those who lay dead in the creek, for the red men had picked up their dead and wounded as they made off.

"Wait!" Joe said.

For minutes a silence that was stunning, after the roaring of so many guns, lay over the scene, while the dust and smoke slowly drifted away.

A hoarse shout broke this quiet. The Kid glanced at the ruined farmhouse and saw Lieutenant Dixon standing with his back against the wall, waving his hat with his left hand.

"Let's get our hosses, boys," grunted the Kid. "Them red devils are likely to come back later on."

Mounted, the three forded the cold waters of the creek and headed toward the Army patrol.

Lieutenant Frank Dixon, walking none too steadily, but holding himself erect as a ramrod, met them. He looked up into the blue eyes of the Rio Kid.

"Oh — it's you, Scout Pryor. Glad to see you."

"Howdy, Lieutenant," grunted the Kid.

Scarecrow California Joe shifted his perpetual tobacco cud from one cheek to the other, and said jovially:

"Why, say, Lootenant, when I seen yuh standin' up there I thought yuh was the Statue of Liberty!"

Frank Dixon, fresh from West Point, was hardly more than a boy, though he sought to hide his inexperience by a strict military bearing. His tunic was spattered with mud and around his right shoulder it was sodden with blood, still he wanted to minimize this wound. The Kid, who once had been a shavetail himself, knew exactly how he felt. Though now that he was a scout, Bob Pryor was no longer subject to the strict discipline and regulations of the Army.

Dixon had a firm chin, a straight nose and a pleasantly wide mouth. Tall and handsome, the Kid thought, and should shake down into a good soldier.

"If he keeps that curly dark scalp of his till he learns the business!" he amended.

"A large party of Indians attacked us without warning," explained Dixon. "I —"

He broke off, and his black eyes widened, horrified as he felt his knees buckling and knew he was about to faint. He fought the weakness, but it was no use. He crumpled in a pitiful heap.

The Kid sprang to his side, knelt by him. With his hunting-knife he cut away a large section of the punctured, bloody tunic, and the shirt under it, to expose the gaping wound between shoulder and neck.

"Shock," he told Joe. "Don't believe it hit the lung. Bones seem all right, too."

A sergeant with three yellow stripes on his arm, a burly Civil War veteran with grizzled hair, galloped over. There were six troopers alive, and two dead. The survivors had minor wounds.

A cross-section from all walks of American life when they had joined, the soldiers had been drilled and trained to fine specimens of manhood by the clever General Custer. The troopers of the Seventh were first-class fighters.

They looked on their dead, now, and on

the slaughtered horses, for which any man of them would have lied and stolen, for love of his horse was instilled in every trooper. Sullen, smoldering rage, desire for revenge was in each heart.

The sergeant, Oley Olsen, stared down at the officer.

"I told him not to come down here, Kid," he said, "but he seen smoke in the sky and figgered he'd save some settler's life. And he would stand up to shoot!"

"He'll learn." The Kid grinned. "See to yore men, Sergeant. We're leavin' here at once."

"Suits me," Olsen agreed, and nodded briefly.

"If I ever get a crack at them red devils, I'll send forty of 'em to their Happy Huntin' grounds for killin' Gertrude," the Kid heard a tall trooper growl. "Why, I loved that horse like she was my own sister!"

That was the general sentiment. The troopers were furious because they could not smash the elusive red enemies who had struck with such cunning stealth. Each soldier was thinking more of his dead horse than of himself, or of the fact that they also would probably be dead if they had not been caught dismounted by the sudden Indian attack as they were investigating the ruins of the smoking farm, where they had found two scalped and pitiful bodies. The only dead troopers were those who had been assigned to hold the horses outside.

The Kid rose up after making a quick job of bandaging Dixon's shoulder in an effort to check the worst of the bleeding.

"Let's see," he said. "We got three hosses — since them riderless mustangs have all run off — and eleven men. We'll take turns, 'cept Dixon. He'll ride my dun, and we'll spell each other holdin' him up. Others hang to stirrups. We'll hafta get out of here quick. Them Kiowas'll be back to check up on us."

"Where'll we head for?" asked Sergeant Olsen. "Camp's twenty miles north, Kid."

"We can make it by dawn if we walk fast."

The sun was dropping to the Wichita Mountains, far westward of their position. It was already reddening, and when the moonlight came, their dust and position would be hidden from spying eyes.

Dixon was propped on the dun, with the Kid supporting the young officer, and they started off, the troopers glad to get out of there. Marching north, they dropped behind the roll of the hill, making all speed they could for camp.

CHAPTER IV
THE MILLER FAMILY

Night fell when they were several miles to the north of the spot from which the Kid had snatched the troopers from death. Pryor motioned toward the wounded young lieutenant.

"He's bleedin' like a stuck pig," he growled to California Joe. "The motion's goin' to kill him, I'm afraid, 'fore we reach camp."

"How 'bout makin' the Miller ranch, Kid? It's five miles west, but we could put Dixon to bed there and mebbe get hosses for the men."

"Good idea."

They switched direction, marching west. It was around eleven at night when they came upon the dark buildings of a Kansas ranch.

Suddenly there came a rifle flash from the house, and they heard lead shrieking overhead.

"Hey, in there!" bawled Pryor. "It's friends, Miller! Let us in."

"Who is it?" came the shouted demand.

"Three of Gen'ral Custer's scouts and a troop of foot cavalry," answered the Kid in a stentorian shout, his white teeth flashing a grin at the sergeant.

Weary and footsore, the soldiers could still smile at their own plight.

A lamp was lighted in the ranchhouse, a roomy structure built of sod bricks and reinforced with timbers from the growth along the Kansas River, which furnished water and sustenance. Always the first settlers sought the stream valleys, since dry land was useless to them.

The band skirted corrals in which were cattle and horses, past a large barn and some sheds, to reach the front door of the house. The lamp cast its glow over the main room, furnished with rough, home-made tables and chairs, and beds. Buffalo and antelope pelts, bearskins and other furs served as rugs and blankets. At one end of the main room was a large fireplace, with arrangements for cooking. Blackened kettles and pots, other utensils, were at hand.

A big man, a splendid, upstanding pioneer, with a shaggy beard and a broad, good-humored face dominated by twinkling, kindly blue eyes, held the lamp as he stood by the open door. His thick hair and beard were touched by the years' rime, and his big nose and wide mouth showed his generous nature. One look at him and an observer was impressed that here was a God-fearing citizen of the best type, a trailbreaker, a family man and the sort who formed the backbone of America. He wore homespun clothing, dark pants and wool shirt open at his hairy throat, and black cowboots.

"Howdy, Miller," drawled California Joe, who knew him. "Sorry to disturb yore pleasant dreams."

Ben Miller grinned at the lean, humorous scout.

"Don't let that worry yuh, Joe," he answered. "We ain't sleepin' none too sound these nights, not with Satanta and Black Kettle on the prowl. They burnt out Smythe's last night, south of here."

The Smythe's, thought the Kid, had probably owned the farm where he had run on Dixon and his men.

Miller's big family was grouped around the main room.

"Yuh know my boy, Andy," he said. "And, gents, this is my wife and daughter, Sue."

Andy Miller, a stalwart youth, stood at his

father's side, gripping a long-barreled buffalo gun. He had Ben Miller's curly hair and sun-seamed eyes, wide mouth and open look. And, standing near the other wall were a woman and a girl that the Rio Kid had already seen as he had lugged in the still senseless Dixon.

Ben's fine wife was middle-aged, her face lined with the cares of a pioneer woman whose work is never done and who labors through unending difficulties. Her hair was smooth on her well-shaped head, and she wore a shawl against the cool of the night.

At Mrs. Miller's side, with an arm around her mother's waist, stood as beautiful a girl as the Rio Kid had ever gazed on throughout his far-flung travels — Sue, the beloved daughter of the household and the eldest of the four offspring of the Millers.

"Why, she's a beauty!" the Kid thought, unable to take his eyes off her.

The men were all staring at the pretty girl. Sue Miller was about eighteen. She had honey-colored, fine-spun hair, and a strong young body. She was of pioneer stock, and of the best blood. Her red lips, parted in a smile of welcome, showed pearly teeth. Her deep-blue eyes held a violet tinge to them, and with her color heightened because of the many admiring eyes upon her, she was

44

startlingly lovely. Hers was a beauty that could not be hidden by the rough homespun clothing she wore.

"A girl like that," the Rio Kid was thinking, as Mireles helped him with Dixon, "is worth the world!"

Sue caught his admiring look, and flushed a bit deeper. The Kid himself was as handsome as a blooded colt, and women never failed to notice him.

"I'll fix some coffee," said Mrs. Miller, turning to the fireplace.

Pryor and Celestino Mireles propped Lieutenant Dixon up between them. Sue's face grew grave as she looked at the wounded officer, saw the blood that had soaked through the rough, temporary bandage.

"Why, he's bad hit," she cried, her woman's heart touched to the core. "Fetch him over here, Mr. —"

"Pryor, Ma'am, Bob Pryor — the Rio Kid," the scout said softly.

Sue ran to smooth a cot at the other side of the room. The Kid deposited the lieutenant gently upon it, while Sue set to work to tend the wounded officer.

"I'd hate to see the Indians hit *this* family," thought the Kid. "They're mighty fine folks." He liked them all — the whole tribe.

They were the salt of the earth.

He saw the two shavers, out of their beds at the noise and excitement. One was about eight, the other taller and two or three years older. From the other room they were watching the uniformed troopers and all that went on, with open mouths and large eyes.

"Hey you, Pierce and Ollie!" called Andy. "Get back to bed, yuh little rascals, or I'll paddle yuh!" He grinned and winked at the Kid. "Can't hold 'em at all. They do as they please."

Pryor stepped over to Ben Miller. "Pack of Kiowas and Dog Soldiers surprised Dixon and his troop," he explained, "when they rode to Smythe's to see what the smoke was. Kilt their horses, and a couple of soldiers, then tried to wipe 'em all out. The lieutenant's bleedin' too bad to be toted farther for awhile. Can yuh keep him here till we send an ambulance?"

"Shore!" boomed Ben Miller heartily. "He's welcome long as he wants to stay. We'll take the best care of him."

Bob Pryor, knowing wounds from his Civil War experiences, knew that the best thing for Frank Dixon was complete rest and immobility. The bullet had emerged from his body, but it had torn nasty, jagged holes. The chief danger was that he might bleed to death. It was much better to leave him here, for the pioneer women had knowledge of first-aid, and could keep him going until a surgeon arrived from the Army camp.

The scouts decided to wait till dawn before resuming their journey to report to Custer. Miller could supply them with mounts, but the troopers needed a few hours' rest.

Hot drink and food accented their full weariness, and they lay down wherever they could and slept. . . .

The Rio Kid was up with the dawn. The gray streaks on the horizon, the fresh autumn air, found him outside tending Saber. Then, as redness tinged the sky, everybody rose. The odor of boiling coffee and frying beef reached keen nostrils.

"Yeah, these are great people, these Millers," the Rio Kid thought.

He strolled back to the long ranchhouse and went inside. Men were stirring all about him. The two boys, Ollie and Pierce Miller, were having a fine time with the soldiers, who were ever kind to children.

Lieutenant Dixon was awake and rational though there was little color in his young face except for a washed-out, yellowish tinge.

47

As Pryor stepped in, spurs jangling softly, Sue Miller was kneeling beside Dixon, giving him a drink of water. Kept in a large jar on a window ledge in such weather, it was cool and refreshing, and Dixon's dark eyes glowed gratefully as he looked up into the girl's lovely face.

"Mornin', Lieutenant," said the Kid. "How'd yuh sleep?" He smiled at the girl.

"Fine, fine," answered Dixon. "I'm — ready to ride."

"No, not today. Yuh've had a bad shock. Ma'am, how's that wound in his shoulder?"

"Doing well. But he shouldn't move yet."

"That's what I figger. Lieutenant, if yuh open it up again yuh may be in the hospital for a month. Take my advice and let me send an ambulance down for yuh from camp."

The young officer was weak, but it was the fear of missing the impending experience as part of the expeditionary force against the Indians that made him acquiesce to the Kid's suggestion.

California Joe, Mireles, Pryor and the troopers were saddling up, preparatory to returning to Generals Sheridan and Custer at Headquarters temporary camp, when two men rode up to Miller's.

"Howdy, boys!" Ben Miller greeted them

heartily. "Say, gents, meet Sam and Charlie Lee, my nearest neighbors. They got a place five miles up the river."

The Lees were men of about forty, bearded, strong of face, blue of eye, with pioneer courage in every inch of them. Sam, the elder, stood two inches over six feet and was that much taller than his brother. Both had sandy hair, big, work-hardened hands, and wore old blue Army overcoats over their work jeans.

"We was down on our south section yes-tidday afternoon and seen a bunch of Kio-was in the distance, Ben," Sam explained. "We come over to see if yuh'd like to fetch yore family to our stockade. We got it ready and figger we can hold off Satanta and Black Kettle and any red gang they want to bring."

Ben Miller shook his head. "Mighty good of yuh, boys. But we got to take care of the ranch. Andy and me can drive 'em off. And Sue ain't a bad shot herself."

Sam Lee bit at his ragged mustache. "Aw right, Ben. I hoped yuh'd come though. We got thirty or forty folks banded together. The way it looks to me, there's due to be plenty trouble in these parts the next month, 'fore the cold weather sets in."

"Yeah, but soon as the snow flies, the

Indians can't move till spring," argued Miller. Like all pioneers he was confident of his ability to defend himself and his own. "I wouldn't want to desert the ranch, Sam."

The Lees did not insist. They went inside and had some hot breakfast. And as they disappeared the troopers rode off, on horses loaned them by Ben Miller. The Rio Kid, Mireles and California Joe waved good-by to the ranch people, and all set out again for the Army camp. The October air was cool, but the sun still felt good to stiff muscles.

They came in sight of the big camp along the river an hour before noon — General Phil Sheridan's temporary post. Tents and wagons were in orderly array; sentries were on duty in company streets. The clear notes of a bugle rang over the rolling, grassy plains.

Half a mile behind the three scouts, on their fast horses, Sergeant Olsen and his squad rolled up the dust as they headed in. Arriving first, the Kid, Joe and the Mexican saw to their horses, left them on the picket line and, with spurs clanking, swaggered toward the Headquarters tent.

General George Armstrong Custer sat in the sunlight on a folding camp-chair, outside the big Sibley canvas. By his side was

General Phil Sheridan, the hero of the Civil War, the greatest general of cavalry boasted by U. S. Grant's victorious army, known all over the world for his bravery and efficiency.

CHAPTER V
THE SCORE

Young Pryor, though not subject to military discipline, being a civilian scout, saluted smartly. Always Custer's magnetic presence thrilled him, and his admiration for the famous Sheridan was deep.

Custer raised his flashing blue eyes. They were keen, with the magnificent spirit and intelligence that animated this brave officer and strategist.

Known as the *beau sabreur* of the Army, Custer's dress was ever startling and unique. In Washington parades, he sported specially designed uniforms of gold and velvet braid. Here on the Plains, in active service, he wore a suit of fringed buckskin, and a wide Stetson from under which his golden curls that were like a lion's mane, fell to his broad shoulders. His high black boots were ornamented with silver spurs. In dress, and in bearing, George A. Custer was tall, and sinewy as a panther.

Born in 1839, Custer had attended West Point, graduating into the Army in time for the Civil War. He had gained promotion with unbelievable rapidity, due to bravery and his genius for soldiering, his work, which he loved. He was a brigadier of cavalry at twenty-three, a major-general at twenty-five.

After the War, when thousands of officers and millions of men were demobilized, the Grand Army broken up, Custer received the rank of lieutenant-colonel in the regulars, a general by brevet.

Assigned to the new Seventh Cavalry, Custer was in fact its colonel and chief, responsible for its *esprit de corps* and fighting power.

Glamorous, a national hero, George Custer continued to grow in stature until, after his untimely death, he became a legend.

Custer smiled on the Rio Kid now, showing even white teeth. He winked at California Joe, who was a favorite and ever a source of amusement with his quaint speech and habits. Joe was a wanderer over the whole immense West, from California to Kansas. Known in the Army camps as a fine scout, he would leave that field now and then to prospect — in the Rockies, the Sierras or the Black Hills of Dakota. But always he would return to his first love — the soldiers.

He was a refreshing character for General Custer, a martinet and stickler for etiquette in Army matters, but at heart a boy, fun-loving, and a great practical joker. Since the old scout was treated as a civilian, however, he was a source of much amusement to Custer.

Back at a lonely Army post waited Custer's beautiful young wife, Elizabeth Bacon Custer. She was with him in spirit, though, ever thinking of him, praying no harm should come to him, for she knew he was ever in the lead of his men, no matter what the danger. Custer adored her, but duty separated them sometimes for months.

Basking in the sun at his feet now were his two great, shaggy staghounds, Blucher and Maida, while two smaller dogs crouched close at hand. Custer loved animals — horses and dogs in particular — and hunting. It all made a pleasant and familiar picture to the Rio Kid who felt most at home in an Army camp. Sometimes, though, it brought a nostalgic longing for old times in the War. Things were different here, however, from those old days of battle. Here, the company streets were spick-and-span, where troopers were busy, caring for their horses, burnishing equipment. Orderlies and aides stood ready for duty. The smell of noonday cooking was in the cool fall air.

The smells, the sounds, the sights in such Army camps had made them the familiar way of life to the Rio Kid. The conical Sibley tents — designed after Indian tepees — set in orderly rows, the bugle calls, the horse detail, kitchen detail and various regular soldier tasks, hardtack and jerked beef and coffee, the huge wagons, painted blue and with sail-like tops, the uniforms, the arms — all massed into a bustling but disciplined picture for the former soldier.

And here with Custer, in this particular Army camp was General Phil Sheridan, the great cavalry chieftain for Grant and Sherman in the War.

Sheridan was in the prime of life now, his beard and mustache still dark, for he was not yet forty. He, too, was a world-famed figure, a friend of crowned heads, of presidents, of the greatest men of his time, among whom he was ranked.

Sheridan, a high-ranking official of the Government, could have remained in Washington, or at some fort in comfort, but he preferred to exchange such ease for the field. Soldiering was his passionate interest, and his shrewd mind had made him a national hero of the stature of Sherman and Grant, famed in song and story.

Phil Sheridan's body was long, as were his arms and legs, though his legs were bowed to fit a horse's barrel. Unlike Custer, he was not a handsome man, his physical characteristics instead rather leaning to the grotesque. He had a round bullet head, and his face was red, weather-beaten. But the Rio Kid knew that behind that stern, composed face was the marvelous brain of a man who, through sheer ability, had never finally lost a battle.

In command of this district, Sheridan trusted Custer implicitly, and would give him unlimited leeway in the matter of action in the field. His nature was altogether grand and unselfish.

"Well, General Custer," said California Joe, shifting his cud, "durned if we didn't spy some redskins when we looked careful."

"Where were they, Joe?" asked Custer. "Hiding in the bulrushes?"

"No, General. They was right out in plain sight. Me'n the Kid was spilin' for a fight but they all run away when they heard us comin'. The Kid and me don't care nothin' for their bullets and arrers. We're like that there settler's gal, she was standin' near the hearth in her bare feet and her ma says,

'Dorothy, there's a red-hot coal under your foot,' and the gal, never movin' says, 'Which foot, Mammy?' "

The group of officers surrounding Custer and Sheridan laughed. Tom Custer, brother of the Seventh Cavalry chief, slapped his leg in glee. An older man, with graying hair and a round, lined, smooth-shaven face, twitched his grim lips. He was Captain Frederick Benteen. An eager young fellow wearing a captain's epaulets, was Captain Louis Hamilton, a grandson of the famous Alexander Hamilton, and also present were Major Joel Elliott, Custer's second-in-command, Captains Thompson, Myer, and West, and Adjutant Cook. They and other stalwart officers on the staff arose at Custer's signal.

Crouched not far away were a dozen Indians in warpaint and feathers — Osages, scouts, friendly to the whites whom they were assisting against other Indians who were running a first-class war against the United States. They stared stolidly at the white officers, unblinking, emotionless, as Sheridan and Custer entered the big tent, trailed by their staff. When the Kid and Joe started to follow, one of the Indian scouts got up and strolled over.

"Hey, Joe — howdy, Kid. How'd it go?"

He grinned at them. He was a gargoyle in appearance, half Negro, half Mexican-Indian.

"Mornin', Romeo," said Joe, grinning back at him. "We still got our hair, ain't we?" Joe solemnly raised his hat to show the thick, tangled mat under it, and the other scout grinned.

Romero, nicknamed "Romeo" by common consent — or most probably because of his hideous features — was a valued man with the expedition, for he had lived among the Cheyennes and Kiowas and spoke their language. He was attached to Custer's regiment as an interpreter.

Leaving him, the Rio Kid and California Joe went inside the tent to attend the council and report.

"General," Pryor said to his commander, "Lieutenant Dixon took a ball through the shoulder in a little brush at Smythe's farmhouse yesterday. We carried him to the Miller ranch, south of here."

"How bad is it?" demanded Custer, his eyes darkening.

"Nothin' serious. He'll need two or three days rest, though."

Custer snapped an order to Captain Hamilton, who hurried to despatch a surgeon to the Miller ranch.

The other officers listened intently to the scouts' report, as it concerned their proposed expedition.

"We've picked the best route as far as the Canadian," the Rio Kid told them.

"How much chance have we of surprising Satanta and Black Kettle, Captain Pryor?" inquired Custer.

"Mighty little just now, General. There are rovin' bands all through the country — Kiowas, Cheyennes, Sioux and Apaches. They're in open revolt, raidin' as they please. Satanta and a black-faced devil ridin' with him, and seventy warriors was the gang that attacked Lieutenant Dixon's patrol. The settlers are in terror for hundreds of miles around. This is the worst they've ever had to stand."

"H'm," grunted Custer, unfolding an official paper. "This, gentlemen, is the score for the past five months of this year: One hundred and sixty-two civilians killed, fifty-seven wounded, forty scalped by Indians. Twenty-four children and six women kidnaped by the Indians. One thousand, six hundred and twenty-seven horses stolen. Twenty-four settlements and ranches utterly destroyed, not including isolated farmhouses."*

"A reign of blood on the Frontier," declared Sheridan.

Custer rattled another paper.

"This," he announced, a sarcastic ring in his voice, "is a report from Indian Agent John Vandon in reply to the many complaints sent in by civilians against Indian depredations. Vandon's post is on the lower Cimarron, in the Nation. He writes: 'I beg to state that the Cheyenne and Kiowa tribes of my district are entirely pacified and none have attacked whites or left the limits of their reservation'!"

Faces reddened with anger at this bald-faced lie, for these officers had seen the mutilated bodies, the burned ruins of homes, and had heard the screams of stricken women and children.

The administration of Indian affairs was under the Department of the Interior at the time, instead of being controlled by the Army. Many post traders and agents were entirely honest men, but there were others who would not risk losing their large and often dishonest profits from dealing with the redmen by antagonizing them in an attempt to control them. While report after

* Note: These figures are official.

report of depredations poured in, such agents insisted that all was serene.

"We all know that such agents value their profits above human life," Sheridan said coldly. "Rather than let the Army in, they watch their charges killing and stealing as they want. We can never hope for co-operation from such a man as this Vandon, for instance. It is now up to the Army, gentlemen."

"Satanta's braves are armed with new breech-loaders," interjected the Kid softly. "Better guns than the troopers' Spencers."

Custer muttered a curse of unrestrained anger.

"Two things must be done, Pryor!" he snapped. "Joe, you listen to this, too. First, I want to know where Black Kettle and Satanta make their permanent winter camp, as soon as possible. And while you two are down that way, check up on Vandon. If you can get any evidence that he's supplying the Indians with any contraband, so much the better."

"They won't settle till the snow flies, General," the Kid said. "Then their mustangs lose flesh and can't move far or fast. Fodder's scarce."

Phil Sheridan nodded complete approval.

"That's true. We can't force a battle for

them in warm weather. Their horses are too fast, and they split up and melt away when we try to strike in force."

"They can't move after the snow sets in," Custer said, "but I can, General. And we should be able to surprise them."

CHAPTER VI
A CELEBRATION

Eagerly the staff officers began planning the winter campaign, an innovation in such warfare. With the Indians immobilized because of snow and the weakness of their mustangs, the troops would have a chance to close in for a decisive battle.

"Joe," Custer said, "we mean to organize our white and red scouts into a special company, and you are chosen to be chief of it."

"Whoopee, General!" shouted California Joe, his blue eyes in their seamy setting sparkling. "That's a great honor, yes, sir!"

So exhilarated was California Joe at being named Chief of Scouts for the expedition that he was walking on air as he stalked the company street at the Kid's side.

"Calls for a real celebration, Kid," he remarked jubilantly, as they went to get some food and spruce up. "In the mornin' we'll start for the south, but tonight the wolf'll howl."

"Better take it easy, Joe," warned the Kid, with a dry grin.

Knowing that no braver and more trustworthy man than California Joe lived when he was on a scout, or if danger must be faced, the Rio Kid was also aware that when no peril threatened and the time came for relaxation, Joe was inclined to do things up brown. It was whole hog or none for California Joe.

Worn out, Bob Pryor went to sleep in one of the Sibley tents after supper. He was roused in the night by loud shouts, and several popping gunshots. Then he heard the confused beat of horses' hoofs. Officers snapped commands, troopers sprang to arms, and a bugle shrilled the alert.

"Indians!" Celestino Mireles exclaimed, grabbing up his rifle.

The Kid snatched at his own carbine and jumped to the slit which formed the door of the Sibley.

Red torches flared up, and lanterns. Dry chips and twigs thrown onto the sentry fires roared to a ruby illumination as the camp sprang to the night alarm. Custer, Sheridan and other officers were popping out of their tents, Colts and sabers raised. Sergeants were bawling order to troopers.

Then, out of the darkness of the plains, galloped a bizarre rider, on a foam-flecked buckskin stallion, tearing full-tilt up Officers' Row. The scarecrow figure stood upright on the animal's bare back, holding on by his toes and guiding the buckskin by a rope hackamore. In his other hand he gripped a pistol which he fired into the air, shrieking at the top of his voice.

"Joe!" growled the Kid, though he couldn't help laughing at the scout's antics. "He's celebratin', shore enough!"

California Joe had peeled off some of his outer clothing, and his hair streamed behind him like a wind-blown mane.

"I'm a wild man from the wildest wilds of the wilds!" he bellowed as he dashed through the camp before the astounded eyes of the officers. "I eat one Indian for breakfast and two for supper! C'mon, yuh red devils, I'm ready for yuh!"

"Bein' named Chief of Scouts proved too much for him," Pryor said to his Mexican partner. "Poor Joe!"

Having consumed a tremendous amount of the raw red-eye available on the Frontier, California Joe was in his own mind leading a charge on a hostile Indian village.

"C'mon, boys, let's clean them vermin out!" he roared.

The Colt flashed in the night, the buckskin sweeping recklessly up the camp street, as troopers and officers alike jumped back from the flying hoofs. Shooting and bellowing, California Joe was on through the camp in a few seconds, disappearing into the darkness on the opposite side.

"He'll be back," the Kid said.

He went into the tent, picked up his lariat. After a few minutes, Joe did come tearing back into the camp.

"Fight! What's the matter with yuh?" he shouted complainingly.

The Kid, behind a tent, waited with his loop. As the tall scout flashed by, he made his cast. It tightened around the buckskin's neck and whipped the animal around, throwing Joe from his precarious perch. The lanky scout hit the sandy earth with a grunt, and before he could rise, the Kid and Mirales fell upon him, disarmed him and forcibly dragged him inside their tent.

"Lie still, yuh danged fool," ordered Pryor, to the struggling California Joe.

General Custer stuck his head inside the slit. His voice sounded stern, although his mustache twitched a bit when he saw the two scouts sitting on Joe's head.

"Bein' chosen Chief of Scouts was too much for him, Gen'ral," Pryor said, grinning. "He'll be aw right in the mornin'."

"He's not Chief of Scouts now," Custer declared. "The job is yours, Pryor. When Joe's sober tell him he's a plain, ordinary, everyday scout from here on!"

"Oh, shucks," muttered California Joe, his fall having thudded some semblance of sanity into his brain. . . .

Reveille woke them, the clear notes of the bugle ringing over the camp. The Kid sprang from his blankets, refreshed by his sleep. He stirred California Joe with a boot toe, and sang softly with the music.

> I can't get 'em up, I can't get 'em up,
>   I can't get 'em up this mornin';
> I can't get 'em up, I can't get 'em up,
>   I can't get 'em up at all.
> The corp'ral's worse than the private, the
>   sergeant's worse than the cor-p'ral.
> The lieutenant's worse than the sergeant,
>   and the captain is worse than 'em all!

"Ugh," grunted Joe, shaking his head, and opening bleary eyes. "My brain's splittin', Kid. What happened? Did some Injun scalp me?"

Gingerly he felt of the matted dark hair on his massive head.

"No, but yuh lost yore job to me," Pryor

told him. "C'mon, we're ridin' south this mornin'."

Complaining and groaning, California Joe made his brief toilet. After breakfast, they saddled up and started for the Indian country. . . .

It was two days later when they rode into Agent John Vandon's Indian Agency post on the lower Cimarron. Spread over the flats in the valley, it was a big depot, serving the Cheyennes and some of the Kiowa tribes.

"Quite a place, quite a place," remarked California Joe. "I was here once afore, Kid."

Pryor's keen eyes swept the rolling site of the post, noting the large log store, and the agent's quarters with its wide front porch. Corrals, in which grazed beef cattle issued by the Government to its wards, the reservation Indians, stood in the rear. There were horses about, some saddled, and Indian mustangs with blanketed backs, decked with gay-hued ribbons braided into mane and tail.

Across the Cimarron stood a couple of hundred tepees. Smoke slowly issued from the hole at the top of each conical hide shelter, lined with warm buffalo robes. Indian squaws, on whose sturdy shoulders fell all the hard labor of life — every task save hunting and making war — were at work, busy as beavers, while red-skinned children played games that mimicked the exploits of their parents.

"Gee-up there!"

Whips cracked like pistol shots in the cool air. To the south of the post showed a U.S. Army commissary train, bound for Fort Cobb, Indian Territory, seventy or eighty miles away. The two dozen large canvas-tops had paused at the agency to repair wheels of the big blue wagons, shoe some of the cavalry escort's horses, get fresh water, and rest. Now it was leaving, escorted by a detail of U. S. Cavalry with a major in command.

As the three scouts rode across the bare central plaza of the agency, one of the mule-skinners driving a Government wagon recognized California Joe.

"Hey, Joe!" one sang out. "How are yuh, yuh old tarantula? Yuh ridin' for Custer?"

"Doggone that big-mouthed Texas Ike," grunted the lean scout. "He'll spill the beans every chance he gets!"

The Rio Kid didn't like it. He had hoped to look around quietly, without exposing their real identity as scouts for Custer. He was frowning as whips were laid on the backs of the long-eared mules and the train started for Fort Cobb, in the wilds of the Nation plunging for the trail, soon to disappear into the woods.

About the store lounged a number of Indian braves, faces solemn yet eagerly expectant for any handout that might come. Blankets were about their hide-jacketed bodies, and feathers in their straight black hair.

About a dozen whites were in sight, here and there, and at one end of the house porch a group of Indian youths squatted, listening to a tall white man who was lecturing to them. The teacher had a book in his hand as he spoke.

"Missionary teacher, I reckon," murmured California Joe, as he, the Rio Kid and Celestino Mireles dismounted.

Joe was considerably chagrined at having been identified by the mule-skinner, Texas Ike, though he knew he and his friends were in no danger from the savages about the trading post. The Indians put on another face when coming in to draw free rations and to barter their furs and other valuables.

The Rio Kid was most interested in the tall, thin man talking to the Indian youngsters. He was the missionary type all right as far as his broadcloth suit, white shirt and string tie went. But his smooth face was red and coarse in texture, a beef-eater's skin, and when he turned his blue eyes on the three new arrivals, nodded and smiled, his large front teeth were his most conspicuous feature.

" 'Ow do you do," he called in a pleasant voice, oddly accented for that part of the country. "Wonderful mornin'."

"Shore is," agreed the Kid, nodding.

The three paused, staring over the porch rail at the class. "Yuh teachin' 'em the Bible, Mister?" inquired California Joe. "That's what them young rapscallions need."

"Yes." The teacher smiled. "But first they must learn English." He came to the rail, held out his hand. "I'm happy to meet you, gentlemen. I am Edward Dobbs, of Manchester, England. A missionary to the savage tribes of North America."

"A beef-eater, eh?" said Joe breezily. "Well, I wish yuh luck, Dobbs. Keeps yore hair on — that's all I got to say."

They shook hands with Dobbs, then strolled on to the store, the center of activity at the post. It was filled with trade goods, cheap trinkets, such as mirrors and flimsy blankets, colored calicoes and ribbons, barrels of condemned salt pork and dried vegetables. And there was little doubt that Vandon also sold high-powered rifles and ammunition to the Indians.

A group of savages blocked the steps, surrounding a slouched giant of a man, wearing dark pants tucked into muddy high boots, a mackinaw, and a narrow-brimmed felt hat pulled low over shaggy hair. He had a bristling black beard, ugly greenish little deep-sunken eyes, and high cheekbones. His skin was cured as though salted and dried in the sun, his nose flat and thick, over his bearded, protruding lips.

"Howdy," he called in a deep bass. "What can I do for yuh, gents?"

"Are you the agent here?" asked Pryor.

"That's me — John Vandon. And you?"

"My name's Pryor," replied the Kid. "This is my pard Joe, and Celestino, we been huntin' buffalo and run outa tobacco." He was still hoping to dispel any suspicion aroused by California's mule-skinner friend.

"Step inside, and the clerk'll oblige," replied Vandon, and plainly the Kid caught the dangerous gleam in the agent's small greenish eyes. However, Vandon sang out: "Hey, Horseface! Take care of these gents."

The Government wagon train was still near the agency, and gunfire might bring the soldiers back.

"Obliged," said the Kid.

CHAPTER VII
CARDS ON THE TABLE

Silently the Indians made way for the Rio Kid and his two companions as they entered the store, in which barrels, boxes and bales stood out in crowded disorder. The smells of brine, stale food, biscuits and damp wool were in the air, and since the narrow windows were covered with thick paper that admitted but part of the light, it was dim.

A man in a canvas apron came to them. He had a long, horse face, adorned with a light-colored mustache and short beard. Under his apron the Kid noted a soldier's faded blue coat, and Army pants stuck into worn military boots. The bulge at his waist was undoubtedly a six-shooter.

"Hello, boys," he greeted. "What'll it be?"

"Tobacco, Mr. — er — what'd yuh say yore name is?"

"I didn't say. But it's Keyes. And you?"

"This is Celestino — Joe — and I'm Bob Pryor. Some call me the Rio Kid. We run

73

outa Navy plug while huntin'."

Horseface Keyes sold them some black Navy plug, which was California Joe's favorite confection. They were hungry for more intriguing food than the dried tough beef strips and hardtack on which they had subsisted during their trip through the Indian-infested Nation, so made some purchases of bread, cheese, and canned goods. That tasted good to the three scouts, as they sat on boxes, eating and then smoking.

An hour passed, during which they chatted with Horseface Keyes about furs and various Frontier matters. Then the Kid said to Mireles:

"Celestino, step out and see to the hosses."

The Mexican lad rose, and glided to the door. The Kid nudged Joe, who caught on, and began by coughing drily.

"Uh — shore is torture, a-ridin' without proper moisture for a man's throat," Joe remarked meaningly.

"Step this way," at once suggested Keyes.

He led them to a large barrel, set on a frame of logs, at the rear of the store. Into a tin cup he let several fingers of smoking whiskey trickle.

"One dollar a throw, gents, special aged in the wood," he said.

"Turpentine, eh?" joked Joe, and drank his off at a gulp. "Oof! That stuff'd burn the hair off'n a brass Indian's chest!"

"We ain't 'lowed to sell it to Indians, brass or otherwise, feller," Keyes reminded sourly.

Both the scouts took that with a grain of salt, for they knew that though once in awhile an inspection took place, that for the most part the Indian agent had full charge, without troublesome accounting of funds and goods furnished by a benevolent government. An agency meant a fortune and was bitterly contested for, by honest men — and others.

"Tryin' to trip me up, are yuh, yuh dirty spy?" an angry voice behind them roared.

The Kid whirled, ducking, as John Vandon, who had come in silently, seized California Joe by the collar and hurled him violently through the air, showing his terrific strength as he lifted the scout as though Joe were an infant.

Bob Pryor quickly took in the half dozen rough looking men who had trailed Vandon inside. All were armed, with coats unbuttoned so they could get at the revolvers strapped to their waists.

Joe, twisting lithely in the air, landed on a cracker barrel, a grunt driven from his body. The barrel overturned and the lean, long figure, padded by the many layers of clothing, was jammed between two large boxes. The loose cover slid off one, and the Kid saw the fine large-bore rifles packed inside it.

They were in a bad spot. If Vandon meant to kill them, it could be done without much trouble, though Pryor had sent Mireles out to see that their horses were ready for a quick getaway. The commissary train was well out of earshot by this time and any reason for putting on an innocent front to fool the soldiers with the train had passed.

Texas Ike had spilled the beans all right.

Vandon, huge fists clenched, bearded chin down, followed up California Joe who was struggling to extricate himself from among the boxes and bales. Joe's wind had been driven from his lungs but he kept his senses, seeking to come up into fighting position. However, his right arm was jammed under him and his pistol was in the holster belt beneath his overcoat.

"Yuh can't fool me, yuh walkin' scissors," shouted Vandon. "I heard what that muleskinner said, and one of my men seen yuh ridin' with Custer! Yuh was sent down here to make trouble for me. I'll rip the hide off'n yore bones!"

The Rio Kid fully realized that an autocrat

like Vandon could easily kill wanderers such as Joe and Pryor. To dispose of their bodies would be simple, and no one could ever call him to account. He had, in fact, only to turn them over to the Kiowas or Cheyennes, whose Dog Soldiers would be delighted to wreak a drawn-out torture revenge on their enemies, the scouts.

Vandon whipped out a large, black-stocked revolver. Red death glinted in the murderous eyes.

The Rio Kid had but an instant in which to act — and knew it.

"Hey!"

That was one of Vandon's gunmen who had followed the giant agent inside. He had seen the lithe Kid digging for his Colt.

A breath later, the tall gunman's pistol roared, the first shot in the sudden melee.

But the Kid, dropping to one knee as he saw the rising weapon of his opponent, felt the slug bite a chunk from his hat crown, and plug into the log wall behind him. Then he had his own gun out and it replied. The man who had tried to kill him took it in the shoulder. A sharp crack sounded, the breaking of bone. The startled gunman gasped in anguish, his gun arm dropping limp.

A thick hogshead offered the Kid shelter on one flank, and his back was protected by the rear wall. A second of Vandon's cronies tried to get him in that instant after his shot, but the Kid's Colt snapped before the gunman's arm was at killing level. The tough's bullet drilled into the rough flooring.

Vandon was startled from his purpose of shooting California Joe. He hesitated and looked back and in that breath as he saw the Rio Kid, smoking pistol ready, white teeth gleaming in the joy of battle, he lost his chance.

"Yuh young guttersnipe!" he shouted, and tried a snapshot at Pryor.

The bullet went wide, and the Kid shot the Colt from the giant's hand. Stung, with blood spurting from his cut fingers, Vandon danced up and down, roaring in pain and rage.

"All right, Vandon!" yelled California Joe. "What'll it be — war or peace?"

The Kid had given him the moments he needed to extricate himself from his embarrassing position and draw, and now, with the older scout up and ready, and with Vandon and two men out of the combat, the odds were more favorable to the Rio Kid.

"What do yuh want?" snarled Vandon, clicking his stained teeth. "Yuh can't get away with this!"

"We're goin' out, and we'll call the scrap off — if yuh don't try to stop us," said Joe. "C'mon, Kid. We'll kill the man who blocks us!"

"Step this way, Vandon," ordered Pryor, gun menacing. "Reckon yuh'll do for a shield till we're outside."

Unwilling, but convinced of the Kid's fighting ability, the burly agent moved closer, fascinated by the menacing black eye of Bob Pryor's Colt, steady on his vitals. The lanky, lithe Joe slid over to his friend. They kept their faces to the main gang, and Vandon helped shield them to the door.

Mireles was on the porch. He had the reins of the three mounts in one hand and a pistol in the other, wanting a chance to help his friends, but not daring to leave his post. The horses meant escape.

"General!" he cried, as he saw Pryor backing out. "Look out! Ees In-di-ans comin'."

The shots had attracted the attention of the savages, and some were curiously pressing in. The missionary, Edward Dobbs, having heard the gunfire and howls of fury in the store, had left his charges and came galloping over, hands raised in horror.

"Gentlemen!" he cried, as he saw the Kid and Joe emerge, guns ready, and with Vandon a hostage. "I beg of you, stop this violence! H'it's a bad example to set our red friends!"

"Dry up, Mister," replied Joe. "We're just defendin' ourselves."

"Take the hosses to the side rail," ordered the Kid.

Joe straddled the rail, and mounted from there. The ticklish moment to ride off had come. The Kid put a foot in the small of Vandon's back and shoved, sending the big agent hurtling across the porch. Then Bob Pryor vaulted the rail, hit Saber's leather and, clinching his legs, gave a warwhoop and spurred after his friends to the rear of the post.

Only wild shots followed them. They made the fringe of woods without being hit.

"Whew!" exclaimed California Joe, wiping perspiration from his face, despite the cold. "I shore don't cotton to that Vandon polecat."

"Acts like he has a guilty conscience," observed the Kid. "We'll ride off now, but after dark we'll come back and check on him. He's sellin' whiskey and contraband to the Indians all right."

"Them galoots hangin' around are mighty tough. Heeled to the eyes, too. And Vandon's got a grip like a cider press."

Ruefully Joe rubbed his strained neck, and

the blue bruises made by the powerful
agent's fingers.

CHAPTER VIII
NIGHT MELEE

It was well after dark when the Rio Kid and his scout companions returned to the vicinity of the post. The red glow of Indian fires was in the vaulted sky and they could see the yellow rectangles marking Vandon's lighted windows.

Dismounting, the two scouts left the young Mexican to hold the horses and keep them quiet, while they crept in, silent as stalking savages, cutting up alongside the agent's house. All was silent for a time, save for the sounds from the Indian village across the Cimarron, and the long-drawn, mournful howls of a distant coyote.

"Here comes a band of riders — Indians," whispered Joe.

They were pressed close against the side of the porch as a large body of savages pulled up in front of Vandon's.

"Father Vandon!" sang out a chief in the van.

By cautiously peeking between the log posts forming the veranda rail, the Kid and Joe could glimpse some fifty redmen sitting their hairy mustangs, bodies blanketed, feathers in their black, braided hair, streaks of paint on their fierce faces.

"War paint!" the Kid breathed.

John Vandon came out, carrying a lamp in one large, hairy hand.

"Howdy, Satanta — howdy, Black Kettle," he greeted. "What can I do for yuh?"

"We need fire water to warm our bones," replied Satanta, "and bullets to warm our new rifles and still the hearts of our enemies, Father. Our friend Black Buffalo said we were to have them."

"Yuh'll get 'em," promised Vandon. "Come on over to the store. But look here, Satanta, and you too, Black Kettle. Yuh want to be careful how yuh show yoreselves, savvy? Custer — Pahuska, Yellow Hair — is on the prod, savvy? He sent a couple of spies down this way. Black Buffalo knows it."

"In three suns we ride, Father," Satanta said gutturally.

"Yeah? Where?"

"On a dog hunt, to the north," replied Satanta.

A stir of amusement went through the

83

gathering, and Vandon grinned, too.

"Give it to 'em!" he shouted.

Carrying his light, the agent strode over to the store, the mounted Indians at his heels, while the Kid and Joe froze in the black shadow of the wall. Soon a large keg of whiskey was rolled out of the store, and fastened to a mustang's back while an Indian mounted to steady it. Two boxes of ammunition followed.

As Vandon passed out contraband to the Indians, another savage, on a powerful horse, thundered by.

"Black Buffalo!" breathed the Kid.

Black Buffalo joined the band with Satanta and Black Kettle. The scouts knew that these three, and their followers, had been largely responsible for much of the horror that dominated the Kansas frontier. Now, without question, they were preparing to start out again on a raid.

Vandon relocked the store, and started back to his house. He was fifty yards from the crouched Kid, who was out in front of California Joe, when Pryor heard Joe whisper hoarsely:

"Cut it out! Get away, dang yuh!"

"Sh!" cautioned the Kid, looking around.

A big yellow hound dog had come up and was sniffing, growling low, and licking at

Joe's face. The lanky scout tried to seize the hound and silence him, but the animal leaped back and began to bark. Other dogs came dashing around the building, all howling and yipping.

"C'mon, let's get!" gasped Joe.

Men began pouring from the house as the dogs set up a terrific din, rushing in to nip at the Kid and Joe as they retreated.

"Who in tarnation's that?" roared Vandon, seeing the scurrying dark figures.

He threw up his revolver and banged away at them, while the other whites, hurrying to that end of the porch, also began shooting after the Kid and Joe. Bullets shrieked in the air, thudded into the dirt as they ran, heads down, for safety.

A man with a lantern in one hand and a pistol in the other suddenly jumped at them from behind the house, blocking retreat. Three more dark figures sprang after him.

"Halt — I'll shoot!" he bellowed.

"It's them two spies!" yelled another of Vandon's toughs.

Vandon heard, came to a sliding stop.

"Hey, Satanta, Black Kettle — Henderson! Come back! This way, pronto! Spies!"

Black Buffalo, Satanta, and the Cheyenne chief pulled their horses up short, whirling, tearing back with a magnificent display of riding, to support the Indian agent. They were trailed by their band of killers.

The Kid knew that these picked braves were part of the organization known as Dog Soldiers on the Frontier. They were men of magnificent physique, all sworn never to make peace with the whites. Riding far and wide, protected by their Indian friends, they created havoc throughout Kansas and Texas and Colorado. With the strongest braves of the Cheyennes, Kiowas, Arapahoes, Apaches and Comanches, they maintained their reign of blood on the Frontier.

The Kid never paused as he ran but, head lowered, butted into the stomach of the man with the lantern, bowling him over, while California Joe fired point-blank across the faces of the trio blocking them.

A quick death by a bullet was far preferable to what would happen if the Dog Soldiers captured them — the scouts knew that. Such redmen were torturers extraordinary, responsible for most of the horror and terror that had come on Kansas. The Kid hated them, knew they must be smashed and their hold broken, or the Frontier would never be safe. Such people as the Millers, and their neighbors, were in horrible peril, with the Dog Soldiers on the warpath. They were sworn to exterminate the white man, sworn to fight to the death.

"If I ever get the chance," the Rio Kid muttered, "I'll nail their hides to the fence!"

To catch such an enemy as Bob Pryor, the white scout, would be a feather in the hair of any Dog Soldier. They would draw out his torture for days, seeking to make him break and show pain or fear. Only by out-matching the Indians in stoic contempt for physical anguish, in shrewder brain and fighting power, could the scouts keep their hair.

The Kid fully realized his danger. He also was aware of what hung upon his getting free — not only his own life, but he stood between the settlers and the red devils who sought his and their blood. . . .

Back at the Miller ranch, Lieutenant Dixon, U.S. Army, was reflecting sadly upon the difference between the theory of war and actual fighting. At West Point, where he had stood high in his class, he had excelled in strategy — on paper. Theoretically, he knew how to maneuver troops in battle formation and force the enemy to a decisive conflict.

He had joined the Seventh Cavalry, full of youthful enthusiasm. With the Indian war spreading like a blazing, murderous inferno that engulfed the whole Frontier, he had expected to do well as a soldier.

Yet in his few weeks with his regiment he had found that the Indians had no intention of standing for a decisive conflict. They eluded the slower mounts of the cavalry, and struck at defenseless settlers. The only occasions on which they would fight were when, far outnumbering the white soldiers, they could bring off a swift and total massacre. If closely pursued, they would split into small groups, spreading far and wide, to meet at some designated rendezvous once they had shaken off the troopers.

On a prosaic fuel detail he had exceeded his orders in riding miles off his trail to see about the smoke in the sky. In so doing he had put his troops and himself into an inextricable position. Only the prompt arrival of the three scouts had saved them all from a horrible torture death at the hands of the Dog Soldiers.

"I'm a fool," he muttered, as he lay on the bunk in the Miller ranchhouse.

"Here, have a drink," Sue's soft voice said.

She was always watching for his needs, and had nursed him gently and carefully through the first shock of the shoulder wound he had sustained in the brush with Satanta's braves. Her hands were skillful and sure in dressing his wound, and did not hurt him.

"Thank you," he said gravely, looking up into her long-lashed eyes.

The Army surgeon had ridden down from Custer's camp, examined and treated his injury. The doctor had agreed with the Kid that Dixon would recover much more rapidly if undisturbed for a few days. He had left instructions and medicine which Sue Miller administered.

"What's wrong?" she asked him, sitting down by his bedside and watching his dark eyes.

"Oh, nothing."

"Yes there is. You're worried."

"I'll tell you," he said, after a moment. "But you mustn't talk about it to anyone."

"I won't," she promised.

"I'm ashamed at having been caught that way. You see, I went beyond my orders from General Custer in going to the Smythe farm. So I was caught. Two men died, and I am wounded. I'm liable to court-martial for that."

"You mustn't feel that way," she said quickly. "You haven't been out here long enough to understand the Indians. And even veterans get caught sometimes. Look what happened at Beecher's Island."

"That's true," he agreed, swiftly remembering.

The story of Beecher's Island was a saga of Indian fighting in Kansas. A fine and experienced Indian fighter, Colonel "Sandy" Forsythe, had, with about sixty frontiersmen formed into a special scout division, ridden into a terrible trap far from possible help. Two thousand Indians had suddenly surrounded them, after they had trailed a small band of savages.

The handful of whites managed to reach a low, sandy islet in the middle of the river, where for a week they held off the repeated and desperate charges of the foe, led by Roman Nose, the Cheyenne chief, head of the formidable Dog Soldiers. Roman Nose and many of his men had died in that epic fight, in which hundreds of Indians felt the bite of white man's lead.

Half of Forsythe's command died or were wounded, the leader himself being badly hurt in the first day's battle. Yet the survivors, eating the putrid meat of their dead horses, behind low mounds thrown up with their hunting knives, had held out until help finally arrived from Fort Wallace. Among others, Lieutenant Beecher, a nephew of the famous Henry Ward Beecher, had met his death.

"If men like that can be caught so," Sue argued, "you can hardly be blamed for riding into a trap. The Indians are clever, especially the Dog Soldiers. Black Kettle has succeeded Roman Nose as chief of the Cheyennes, and Satanta is as fiendishly smart as a wolf."

These people of the Frontier knew the Indians. Those safe in the East could not imagine the horror and sufferings of outlying settlers. . . .

His youth, and health had made it possible for Dixon to throw off the shock quickly. His lacerated flesh was healing well and it would not be many days before he could be taken in an ambulance to the Army camp.

Sue was studying his boyish, dark eyes and the curly, black hair she had freshly brushed for him that morning. He was very young, she thought, and because her Frontier life had matured her beyond her years, she had a maternal feeling for him as he lay helpless in her home.

Dixon suddenly smiled at her, with a flash of the even white teeth in his handsome face. He was grateful to the Millers, all of them, for their kind care of him. Mrs. Miller cooked for him what delicacies she could get, and the rancher was hearty and bluff, cheery. The stalwart Andy, about Dixon's own age, was forthright and likable. The two younger children, Ollie and Pierce, tow-headed, bare-footed and light-hearted, played around Dixon's bed, in the big main room of the house until their mother or elder sister shooed them outside.

But the girl — Sue. The young lieutenant could not classify his own thoughts about lovely Sue Miller.

CHAPTER IX
AN IDYLL OF THE PLAINS

Always there was work around a Frontier home. Bread to be baked, water to be carried, wood to be fetched, clothing to be made or mended. As the days passed, it seemed to young Lieutenant Dixon that Mrs. Miller was never at rest from the crack of dawn until the family retired.

The rancher and Andy, sometimes aided by the smaller boys, had tasks that kept them out most of the daylight hours. Sue helped her mother, seeming never to tire. Yet she managed to dress cleanly and neatly and her pretty light hair was never awry. Dixon came to admire them all deeply for their industry and good cheer.

One night, when nearly a week had passed while the young Army officer had been cared for by the Millers, the big rancher, Ben Miller, came in, a grin on his bearded face.

Andy trailed his father inside. Both were

covered with dust, their faces grimed, for
they had been working all day with cattle.

"Howdy, Frank!" sang out Andy. "Yuh're
lookin' mighty pert. Soon yuh'll be able to
ride on the trail of them red devils that shot
yuh."

The little ones were eating cornmeal
mush, sitting by the fire of blazing chips,
used as fuel all over the plains country. Mrs.
Miller was fixing a meal for her menfolk.
The odor of frying pork, and of coffee
pervaded the dim-lit ranchhouse, cozy with
its hung buffalo and antelope robes. Outside
a fall wind whistled about the corners.

"I'll have a bite," said Andy, "and then I'll
be startin', Ma."

"You be careful on the trail, Andy," his
mother cautioned, looking at him anxiously.

"Aw, I can fool any red rascal that ever
rode the plains," boasted Andy, winking at
Dixon.

"Where you going, Andy?" inquired
Dixon.

"I'm drivin' some beef cattle to sell to the
soldiers," Andy told him.

"Just a small bunch," Ben Miller added.
"The fewer stock we got around now, the
better. It ain't such a bait for the Injuns."

"Going alone?" asked Dixon.

"Pierce is goin' along," replied Andy.

Pierce, the ten-year-old, looked embarrassed as all eyes turned on him. Yet he was proud to be doing a man's work in helping his brother.

"Pierce can drive cattle as well as any cowboy yuh ever met, Lieutenant," Andy observed. "He's a real hand."

"Isn't it dangerous?" Dixon demanded. "With the Indians out?"

Andy shrugged. "Night's the time. We'll be 'most to the camp by dawn. Back home in four days."

As soon as Andy had eaten, he and Pierce went outside, Ben helping start them off. Dixon heard the sounds of hoofs dying away, then Ben Miller came back inside, and sat by the fire, taking off his leather windbreaker and heavy cowboots, and filling his old black briar pipe. He smoked calmly for awhile, finally repairing to the lean-to where the family slept, since the main room had been given over to Dixon.

The next day Sam Lee, the neighbor who had begged the Millers to come to his fort up the river, rode into the yard and dismounted. Through the window, Dixon heard Lee talking to Ben Miller.

"Looka here, Ben, whyn't yuh come over till the rumpus dies down? It's gettin' worse, I tell yuh, 'stead of better. We got sixty folks

95

there now and can hold off an army of Injuns. Reason I come today was to tell yuh that a friendly Osage stopped at my place last night and said that the Dog Soldiers are plannin' a bangup raid in these parts. Satanta, Black Kettle, and the lot of 'em mean to clean the district."

"Well, I dunno, Sam," Miller replied in a troubled voice. "If I leave the ranch unguarded, they'll burn it shore. That means I lose everything I got without even a fight. I reckon I can hold 'em off. If it gets too hot, I'll come to yore fort."

"Better come now," urged Lee.

"I'll hafta wait till Andy and Pierce get back. Then I'll come."

Dread hung over the entire Frontier. The vigorous raids of the Indians kept the settlers in continual trepidation. The tall, rangy Lee who was one of those deeply feeling it came inside for a bite to eat and a word with Mrs. Miller and Sue. Dixon watched him as the grim-faced young rancher eyed Sue. Charlie Lee was married but this Lee brother, Sam, was a widower, his wife having died the previous year.

A troubled sensation which he could not understand gripped Frank Dixon's heart. But he did understand that when Sue smiled at Sam Lee, he didn't like it.

But Lee did not stay long. He had too much to attend to at the fort he had constructed near his home, where now were gathered the settlers who preferred to band together during the Indian trouble. Sam Lee soon rode back to his ranch.

In the middle of the following morning, an alarm was sounded, and Miller came to the door.

"Bunch of riders comin' from the north, Ma. Ain't shore yet whether they're Injuns or not."

He took a post, rifle at his side, by the small window in the big main room, watching the dark line on the flat plain. It was half an hour before he relaxed, and announced, with a grin at Dixon:

"Soldiers, with an ambulance. Reckon they're comin' for you, young feller."

Eight-year-old Ollie went galloping out to see the troopers coming up. Ben and his wife stepped to their yard to welcome them. Sue stayed at her task, baking bread in a Dutch oven. She did not look around at Dixon.

"Sue," he asked, "will you give me a drink of water?"

"Yes," she said, her voice low and husky.

She came to him with the tin cup and propped up his head so he could drink. But when she tried to leave he seized her hand and held her.

"Will you miss me?" he asked. "You've been very good to me."

For a time she would not meet his eyes.

"Look at me," he ordered.

"Yes, I'll miss you," she said. "I — I never knew anyone like you before. You're different from — from the others."

"Such as Sam Lee?"

"Sam's a good man," she said quickly.

"Certainly he is. A splendid fellow."

In the distance came the creak of wheels, the jangle of accoutred cavalrymen.

"Will you kiss me good-by now, Sue?" begged Dixon.

She bent over him, and he felt the warmth of her full red lips pressing against his. Then she jumped up and ran outside.

It was not long until the troop of cavalry rode up to the yard. Captain Tom Custer, brother of the general, was in command. The surgeon, Dr. Lippincott, was with the ambulance.

The tall Custer came inside, stooping to enter the low door. He was handsome in blue tunic, cavalry Stetson, spurred black boots and corded trousers. His Army pistol was strapped at his waist, and his saber hung from its belt.

He grinned jovially at Dixon.

"Well, Dixon, I've come to take you home!" he sang out. "How are you?"

"I'm fine, sir."

The surgeon entered, quickly looked over the wounded officer.

"He can stand the trip, Captain," he announced.

Troopers entered with an Army stretcher. Dixon, wrapped carefully in warm blankets, was gently lifted to it, and loaded into the mule-drawn ambulance. The surgeon got inside with him. Tom Custer had around fifty men with him, armed with saber, carbine and pistol. It was a large escort, thought Dixon, as Sue waved to him and he waved back.

Then he heard Captain Custer speaking to Ben Miller.

"If you wish, Miller, we'll escort you and your family to safety. Our Osage scouts report that a large body of Indians under Satanta and Black Kettle are planning a big raid out this way. We hope to meet them, but you know how slippery they are. My orders were to pick up Lieutenant Dixon and offer you an escort to a place of safety. I can wait an hour for you to throw some things together, if you'll come."

"Thanks a-mighty, Cap'n, but if I go

anywhere it'll be to Sam Lee's. They got a fort there and plenty men. . . . Did yuh see anything of my boy, Andy? He drove some beeves to yore camp."

"Yes, he came in with the cattle safe and sound. He was lucky to slip through, Miller, because the country's alive with parties of raiding Indians. They're so bold no small group is safe traveling the plains. They hit an emigrant train fifty miles west of here three nights ago, wiped out every man, woman and child in it, and burned the wagons. And even on our way down here — General Custer wished Dixon brought in at once because of the increasing danger — a band of Arapahoes fired on us. I wish you'd come to the camp with us, sir."

"I reckon when Andy shows up, we'll all go over to Lee's," Miller said thoughtfully, then added, "How is it my boys didn't ride home with you?"

"Our quartermaster's away, on a trip to Fort Dodge and back with a train of supplies. Your son wished to wait until he returned, so he could collect the money for the cattle. He asked me to tell you that he'd be home in a few days."

Ben Miller nodded. "He's a right smart lad, is Andy."

"You won't come, then?"

Miller's eyes swept the comfortable ranch which, by his own and his family's hard labor, had been carved from the wilderness. He shook his head.

"Not now, Cap'n. Mebbe later. Thanks agin."

"Better come," called Dixon, but Miller was obdurate.

The dashing Tom Custer sang out an order, taking the reins of his magnificent charger from his orderly. Another officer, young and slimly handsome, with an eager, boyish face, rode up.

"All ready, Hamilton?" asked Captain Custer.

Louis Hamilton, grandson of the great Alexander Hamilton, reported all ready. He was a capable officer of the Seventh Cavalry, despite his little experience at Indian warfare. Both Custer and Hamilton were intrepid, valuable Army men, of fighting blood and tradition. The two men were close friends.

Frank Dixon's eyes were alight as he looked out of the ambulance window. Everything was in splendid order. Sabers and carbines were gleaming; leather neat. All the horses in the troop were grays, one of General Custer's ideas, to improve the looks of his companies by assigning mounts of the same hue to each troop under his command.

At the order, a bugler blew "To Horse!" The tanned, hardened, well trained troopers stepped to the heads of their steeds. "Prepare to Mount" rang out, then "Mount," and as one man the troopers were in the saddle, formation of two lines along each side of the ambulance.

"March!"

The bugle relayed the order, and they were on their way.

Frank Dixon stared at the little family group formed by the Millers, whom he had grown to like so much, and to whom he was grateful for the kind care shown him. Sue waved to him, smiling. But Custer's news of the Indians worried Dixon. He wished the Millers had come along with the escort.

As the ambulance drew away, he could look back through the faint haze of dust that rose from hoofs and wheels and see them still standing there, the little boy in front, his eyes wide at sight of the soldiers, the stalwart pioneer with one arm thrown about his wife's shoulders. Sue stood apart, a short distance from her parents.

Dixon felt his heart clutch at sight of the settler family standing there before their beloved home. They lived roughly, braving the elements, fighting drought and cold, the power of Nature. Their fare was simple and rough, their clothing and furnishings crude. Life was a hard, unending struggle, but these people were pioneers who had come to Kansas so they might be free, might be able to own and live on their own section of land, the chief tangible wealth of the nation.

CHAPTER X
RED PERIL

Riding on at a pace accommodated to the plodding mules drawing the ambulance, the company of troopers left the belt of timber along the creek behind them. For mile after mile the rolling plains seemed flat as a pancake. Lines of troopers were on either side of the creaking wheeled vehicle.

Captain Hamilton had the advance, with a dozen seasoned troopers scouting the way. The short grass of the plains, sustaining the buffalo and antelope, and smaller ruminants, was crisp and brown in the cool of the autumn.

Then Hamilton saw something far off to the west. The company kept moving, as Tom Custer took his field-glasses from their case and strained his eyes that way.

"A herd of buffalo," he reported.

Several more miles rolled off. The sun was warm, though the wind that had a clear sweep across the plains was chilling.

Wrapped in blankets, with the odor of the doctor's pipe in his nostrils, Dixon nearly dropped off to sleep with the swaying, gentle motion of the ambulance.

Still the plains ahead seemed absolutely deserted, flat as a billiard table. It did not seem possible that a rabbit could hide within miles.

Yet suddenly half a dozen mounted Indians appeared as by magic, just outside carbine range, and rode across the face of the advance guard, whooping and yelling like madmen, giving a magnificent and unsurpassable display of horsemanship.

Hamilton let the main company close up, and Tom Custer rode out to join him. Dixon, awakened by rifle shots, heard the two officers talking.

"They must have come out of a ravine," Hamilton remarked.

"No doubt."

Cut into these great wild plains were innumerable large and small ravines, the water courses in rainy seasons, but dry at other times of the year. These the Indians used in place of timber for cover. It was often possible to travel through these ditches for miles without breaking the surface of the plain.

On their hairy, swift mustangs, the half

dozen braves defying the troop of cavalry came closer, shrieking wildly. As they came within rifle shot, they began firing at the soldiers, and slugs whistled overhead.

Tom Custer spoke with an Osage Indian, a scout assigned to his company. The Osages, decimated by tribal wars with the Sioux, the Comanches and Cheyennes, were friends of the white man and content to live within his protection. This Osage scout, tall and broad-shouldered, clad in buckskin, feathers and paint, could speak a little English.

"Hold 'em off," Custer ordered.

Troopers dismounted, knelt to fire at the swift-riding savages.

"What tribe?" Custer asked the Osage scout.

The Osage drew his hand across his throat. "Sioux."

"Bold as brass," remarked Hamilton.

The troopers were peppering away at the shrieking Indians, whose trained war ponies zigzagged as they flew over the plain. Clinging to the far side of their horses, with only a foot and head visible to the troopers, the savages shot over the manes of their mounts.

"Let me take a dozen men and chase them into the ground," Captain Hamilton begged.

Tom Custer shook his head. "No, Hamilton. You know their game as well as I do. They've probably got two or three hundred braves hidden in a cut a few miles from here. . . . Forward! Bugler, sound the march!"

The company resumed its steady march, with troopers firing from their saddles. One Indian, riding like a mad centaur, ventured too close and Hamilton's revolver shot killed the horse. The savage rolled head over heels in the grass and, as Hamilton spurred out to try to capture him, one of his comrades came tearing in. Without losing speed, the dismounted Sioux leaped up behind his friend, and they rode off full-tilt.

Captain Tom Custer was right. They had marched but a half a mile when a large body of Indians appeared as by magic from the plain to their left. There were nearly two hundred, and the Osage said they were Sioux.

"I wish we could come up with 'em, Louis," Custer growled.

"Me, too," Hamilton said yearningly.

But for too long the Army had been bested by the Indians. They had learned they could not overtake the savages, who had grown so bold they would beard troopers in broad daylight, seek to cut off a rear guard or draw a small pursuing party into ambush. Now the Indian-band shrieked insults, and sent clouds of bullets and arrows at the moving soldiers, but did not approach too closely.

Holding them off, Tom Custer and Hamilton continued their march toward camp. . . .

Only because it was night could the Rio Kid and his mates — Celestino Mireles and California Joe — embattled at Indian trading post, elude the first heated, savage charge of their red pursuers.

Saber was more than a match for the Indian horses, but there were fast steeds among those ridden by the savages, who were expert at judging horseflesh. An Indian would barter his belongings, his tepee, his squaw and his children, even his gun, but he would never part with his favorite war pony.

There was timber down here in the Indian Nation, and rocky ground. The three scouts fled into nearby woods as they sought to keep ahead of the fierce devils on their heels.

"Funny, I was sorta chilly a while ago," remarked California Joe. "Now I feel hot all over, Kid."

The Kid dropped back a few yards, to slow pursuit and allow the slower animals of his friends to draw away. Pistol in one hand, he waited for the van of the Indians who were spread out in a wide line, to sweep the woods for them.

Half a moon gave light, too much light to suit Pryor. Only a couple of hundred yards behind he could hear the sounds the foe made as they came through the forest.

"Yeah, it is hotter'n we figgered, in these parts," he muttered. "But if I get back to Custer he'll know where these Dog Soldiers and the war tribes get their guns and ammunition. That Vandon's a skunk if ever there was one — hand-in-glove with Satanta and Black Kettle, eggin' 'em on in their war against the whites! And for big profit."

The quickest way out had been through the woods. They dared not cross the river in the moonlight so close to the Indian village. Besides, there was an open plain that way, and they must have concealment.

For three miles they kept on, dodging behind rock outcroppings, or for patches of timber that would give them a few more minutes in which to gain on the dogged pursuit. And only the night made this method of escape possible.

At last, with their horses lathered, they reached a small brook. Leaping from their saddles, and leading their mounts, they took to the water, wading to their shins and knees, seeking to cover their trail for a time.

After half a mile of this very difficult progress, slipping on rounded stones in the brook's course, they paused to listen. They heard the purling of the water, then the cry of a distant night bird came to them.

"Hear that?" breathed the Kid, ear cocked.

"Yeah, I hear it," replied Joe. "They've cut us off, Kid, on the north."

They knew that bird call they had heard was an Indian signaling. And they caught the answer, from the east of their position.

"We'll double, boys, and try to work past to the south of the agency, then back the route we come down."

"It's the only way," agreed Joe.

They left the water and rode west, bearing a bit south so they could pass out of sight of Vandon's clearing on the Cimarron. After a time they struck another small affluent of the river, and waded once again, not daring to stop.

CHAPTER XI
HIDDEN VILLAGE

Dawn's first touch forced the Rio Kid and his fugitive companions to hide. In dense thickets they left their tired horses, muzzled against any possible sound the animals might try to make. Then, carefully brushing out any slight marks they made with the moccasins which all three of them now wore, they crept up on a red rock bluff that was fringed with brush.

They had been there about an hour, two dozing while the third kept watch, when the Kid, on duty, suddenly saw two lithe Dog Soldiers slide up not ten feet from him. And not a sound had come to his keen, trained ears!

They were men of Black Kettle's band, tall, powerful, red warriors. Their faces were painted for war, in streaks of yellow, vermillion and black, designed to make their aspect even more terrifying to their foes. Braided in their black, pattern-shaved hair were eagle feathers. Both wore fringed deerskin pants, hide shirts, and had revolvers and scalping-knives tucked in their belts. They carried breech-loading Springfield rifles, and their pouches bulged with ammunition.

One had a tomahawk or war hatchet in his sinewy red hand, and each sported half a dozen dried scalps at his belt — scalps of white people, chiefly, but after the skin had been stretched and dried, the scalps had been dyed various colors, yellow, blue, red.

High of cheekbone, curved noses dilated, the two Cheyennes paused close under the flattened-out Pryor, conversing in the sign language. Then the man with the hatchet stooped and sniffed at the ground.

Pryor put a soft hand on California Joe's cheek and eyes. Joe awakened without a sound.

The second Dog Soldier was casting about to the left of his comrade, and the Kid knew he could take no chances. He held up his left hand to California Joe, and both white men drew their long knives.

The Cheyenne with the hatchet signaled his mate, who came silently to him. Squatted under the rock bluff, they studied the slope up which the trio had crept earlier.

The Indian scouts had smelled them out.

Pryor had but a second or two in which to act. With a nod to California Joe, the Kid launched himself, striking down with all his might as he hit on top of the Indian on the right. California Joe's long body landed on the other brave.

The struggle was over, with hardly a gurgle out of their prey. Both scouts knew how to kill when they must. They arose from the twitching bodies of their foes.

"We got to sashay outa here, Joe," the Kid said grimly.

They saddled up and started stealthily south. They dared not remain where they were, for more Indians would be along and find the bodies of the slain red scouts.

Sunlight streaked down through the openings of the forest, but trees shadowed the trail the ever alert Kid picked. They had gone but a quarter mile when he glimpsed a savage as the Indian leaped behind a tree trunk. He fired, his revolver flying to his hand with magic speed.

Half a dozen painted warriors sprang up and began shooting as the three white scouts veered right and rode at full-tilt.

Warwhoops rang in the forest. They seemed to be answered from every direction.

"Shoot through, boys!" ordered Pryor,

spurring on.

Revolvers in hand, the three rode for it. They splashed across a creek, and a bullet whirled within an inch of the Kid's bent head. He replied, putting a slug through the shaved pate of a Kiowa brave who had sought to bring him down.

The pistols of Joe and Mireles were snapping fury at a dozen braves who leaped at them, shrieking their hate. For moments it was hot and heavy. Then the white men were through, leaving behind them the writhing bodies of four wounded savages.

California Joe and the Mexican had felt the burning bite of enemy lead but neither was seriously hurt. Blood streamed from the tall scout's leathery, bearded cheek as he grinned at the Kid.

"Felt like a wasp stung me, Kid," he remarked. "Ever hear the story of the bee and the —"

Shrieks told them that reinforcements to the Indians they had smashed through were coming up. Their horses, slightly rested by the halt, tore on.

Running, fighting off a few braves who managed to get within gunshot distance, they kept on through the whole day, forced on south, away from Kansas, by their implacable enemies. It was not until dark fell that they finally shook off the pursuit and, utterly exhausted, went into camp thirty miles southwest of Vandon's agency post.

"Now what?" growled Mireles, throwing his bony body on the cold earth.

"Drink, food, and sleep," the Kid replied.

They had cold jerked beef and hardtack in their saddlebags, but the Kid, feeling the need of something warm, decided they must risk a fire, which he built of twigs in the shelter of an overhanging rock. A handful of ground coffee thrown into boiling water made a delicious drink.

After a brief nap of about two hours, they rode on through the night, this time in a westerly direction, so as to circle well around their enemies and make for Kansas.

It was close to midnight when Joe paused.

"Hear that, Kid?" he asked.

They listened. The wind from the northwest brought on it a low, throbbing hum, and distant yells.

"Indian village," observed Pryor.

"And a big 'un."

"Our main job for Custer was to locate the secret villages of the Cheyennes and Kiowas," the Kid growled. "I'm goin' up. You boys keep on this line and I'll meet yuh in the Antelope Hills."

"As you say, Kid," the older scout said.

"Keep yore hair on."

Bob Pryor cut up toward the far-off noises he had caught. Indians such as Satanta and Black Kettle, Kiowas, Cheyennes, Comanches, Sioux, always cunningly and cleverly kept the sites of their winter homes a secret from the white man. This was because they were unable to pick up and flee, or move about from day to day as they did through spring, summer and autumn when hunting was good and pasturage for their ponies might be found anywhere.

After the snow fell, the savages unfriendly to the whites retired to the fastnesses of the forests and with their stores of jerked buffalo meat from the fall hunts, lasted out the long winter. To discover the exact sites of such villages would be a military secret of the first order, and one which Custer would be eager to know.

So the Kid kept on, winding through the rocky lanes of the woods, crossing feeders and creek, drawing ever closer to the sounds. At last as he dropped into a wide, wooded valley, a red glow through the trees sent him off Saber. He left his reins on the earth, patted the dun, cautioning him to stand quiet.

Then, silent, he crept toward the Indian village.

It was a big one, and red bonfires lit the scene. Long lanes of tepees, built of spruce poles and buffalo hides, stood on the bank of the stream in the sheltering valley. Dogs howled — the ever-present mongrels to be found about an Indian village. A bell tinkled on the grassy flat, where hundreds on hundreds of indian ponies grazed.

Straining his keen eyes, the Rio Kid estimated the numbers of painted, feather-decked braves dancing and carousing around the big fires. They were shouting and boasting, war-dancing.

"Black Kettle — Satanta — Black Buffalo," he muttered, picking out the figures of prominent chiefs.

Guns, rifles and pistols, knives, bows and arrows were thick as fleas in the camp. Whole deer carcasses and great joints of buffalo meat roasted on the spits. Barrels of whiskey were being tapped. It was a tremendous occasion, and the Kid guessed there were around two thousand Indians in sight.

"Winter camp, shore as shootin'!" he decided, hugging himself, for it was no mean feat to locate such an enemy base. "And they're gettin' ready for a big foray! That checks with what I heard Satanta say to Vandon, though I didn't figger it was as bad as this! Why, they'll wipe out the whole

117

Frontier with that gang!"

Not only could he identify the wild Cheyennes, by their feathers and tribal marks, but also the large groups of Kiowas — Satanta's people — Arapahoes, Comanches, Sioux and Apaches. These were the tribes who were making most of the trouble in the land.

Having checked the great winter depot, well-hidden in the forests of the river valley, he returned to Saber and rode on toward the Antelopes. A couple of miles on he sighted another campfire, and discovered a second large village where a couple of hundred lodges stuck their dark points to the night sky. And, farther along, he discovered a chain of Indian camps.

It was the vital information which General Custer needed to complete his plans for striking a crippling blow at the raiders!

The Kid pressed on toward the Antelope Hills, riding a wide circle to avoid bumping into any of the Indians teeming in the wooded bottoms. . . .

Back at the Indian agency, John Vandon cursed hotly as party after party reported that the three men who had spied on his post had not yet been taken.

Black Buffalo finally came in and admitted that the Rio Kid, California Joe and the

118

Mexican had managed to slip through the savage cordon drawn about the woods for miles around the agency.

"Just come from Black Kettle's village," Black Buffalo growled. He seized the whiskey bottle to warm himself after the swift ride through the frosty air of the dark hour before dawn. It was already cold enough for the ground to be frozen hard, although snow had not yet fallen. "I've got 'em worked up to killin' pitch, Vandon." He let the fiery liquid gurgle in his throat.

"Custer's on the march, Henderson," growled the giant agent. "Them three that was here come to spy for him. They caught me passin' whiskey and ammunition to Satanta and Black Kettle. If they get to Custer, it'll likely be my ruin here."

"They'll never have a chance to talk! We'll catch up with 'em." Black Buffalo swore a hard oath. "What we need is a spy in Custer's force. Custer's enlistin' Kansas volunteer cavalry, and we'll send a man to join up. I've got this big attack by the Indians all set, and it'll bring the Army down with all four feet. They'll hit so hard, the savages won't recover for years!"

"What good'll that do us? Plenty of settlers in south Kansas'll still be alive and kickin'. And when the soldiers beat the

119

Indians, white men'll pour in thick as fleas!"

"Of course they will. All the better for us, because by then we'll own the best land and the key points. There'll be a railroad through southern Kansas for certain, hookin' up to our mines."

"Yuh'll hafta work fast. I tell yuh, I own a nice thing here, makin' plenty, but it looks like I'll lose it, thanks to you."

Black Buffalo's hard eyes drilled the agent.

"Don't be so crusty, Vandon! We'll be kings of the Frontier. We're headin' right now to attack the settlers on the ranches and farms we want for control. Satanta's scouts report that many of 'em are collected at Lee's ranch, and we'll hit it and wipe 'em all out. I want Miller's place, too. A wholesale massacre like that'll hurry the Army into full war against the Indians and we'll have won. I've got Black Kettle and Satanta fooled. They believe I'm with 'em all the way!"

Murderous plans were working out like clockwork. Black Buffalo, the evil core of the business, was driving the Indians into a suicidal mass attack on southern Kansas. Emboldened by a number of successes, against settlements and outlying ranches, at cutting off small soldier patrols, the Dog

Soldiers would strike with all their horrible
might.

Chapter XII
Red Raiders

Broad daylight had arrived when the Rio Kid saw below him the red, winding bed of the Canadian River, and the strange terraces of the Antelope Hills dropping down to the valley level. Of porous sandstone, they stuck up as high as three hundred feet into the blue sky, bizarrely shaped sentinels over the Kansas plains. The dried brown leaves of the stunted trees following the snaky river line rustled in the breeze, and a thin coating of ice gleamed in the backwater pools.

He was now miles away from the great Indian villages he had spied out for Custer. He held information that would greatly facilitate the general's campaign plans, information concerning the hidden enemy's position that was invaluable to the Army.

His eyes hunted from the plateaus for signs of his friends, who were to meet him near here. Not seeing them he camped for a time, resting, having a cold snack and a drink, letting Saber recover from the grueling run.

Then the dun shivered, pushed a soft muzzle to the Kid's hand. Pryor arose, straining his eyes to the south. Two riders had come into sight, slowly weaving toward the Antelopes.

He identified his friends. They had traveled a more roundabout course than the Kid, he discovered, when they soon reached him.

California Joe was in fine fettle, grinning very broadly as he greeted Pryor.

"What's the name of the river we crossed half an hour 'fore we split?" the Kid asked. "The Washita?"

"Yeah — the Washita. Runs into the Canadian finally. Why?"

"Black Kettle, Satanta and the whole crew're camped on it, forty miles down."

"Yuh don't say! Custer'll shout his head off when he hears that, Kid."

"Well, we'd better be ridin'. I figger the lid's due to blow off the Frontier any minute, Joe."

They rode into the valley of the Canadian. Crossing a small feeder brook, California Joe, ever on the lookout for precious minerals, swore and cried:

"Hey, wait a jiffy, Kid! I see some gold — and silver, too! By heck, it's thick as coffee in a mill!"

The Kid glanced at the clear waters, spied the yellow and lighter sheen of the metals.

"No time now, Joe," he insisted. "We'll come back when we ain't so pressed. C'mon. We got to reach Custer 'fore them red devils strike."

They swam the Canadian, breaking the thin layer of ice, and headed on for Kansas at full-tilt when they came onto the flats.

On the plains, they could see and be seen for many miles. Knowing the plans of the Indians, the Kid kept a sharp watch. It was not long until he saw a faint roll of dust off to the right, and with his two comrades hastened to hide in a nearby ravine.

From this shelter they finally spied a large band of mounted Indians, and were forced to remain in hiding for hours.

"Better wait till night," cautioned Joe.

They took turns sleeping. After dark, they resumed their march for Custer's Kansas camp.

Dawn found them only a day's ride from it. The plain seemed clear and the Kid, anxious to reach his commander and report, decided to keep on for a couple of more hours.

"Look!"

Celestino Mireles, who had glanced behind, gave a cry of alarm. The Kid quickly turned in his saddle. Out of the earth, it seemed, though Pryor knew it was from a big ravine, had appeared a huge band of savages. They were heading rapidly to cut off the three scouts.

"Ride!" urged Joe.

Spurs dug in, the trio tore over the grassy flats. The Indians shrieking and whooping it up, rode after them.

"Must be two hundred of 'em!" grunted Joe as he jounced in his leather. "That's Black Kettle leadin' 'em!"

The ground flew under the hoofs of the horses. The Kid glanced back.

"They're pickin' up on us, boys!"

"Head for the Miller ranch — right over the next slope," panted California Joe.

The Indians were on fresh horses. Their riding was masterful, and they came at breakneck speed after the scouts, gaining yard after yard, until they were within carbine range. Some of them stood up on the flying mustangs to shoot after the white men.

The Rio Kid might have outridden the Indians on Saber, but he would not desert his two friends. Mireles' horse was still going strong, but Joe's was failing.

They came up over the long crest of the plainsland wave and saw the Miller ranch. Smoke was rising into the sky.

"We can make it!" cheered California Joe. "There she be, boys! We can hold 'em off in there —"

The Rio Kid, breasting the rise, stared at the ranch.

"What the —" he shouted.

The gunshots, the yells of the Indians, smote the crisp Kansas air. To the south, his keen eyes glimpsed rolling dust — another large band of savages moving away.

They swept up to the ranch, but the house was a smoldering ruin, roof caved in, the barn a heap of burned timber, and sod bricks crumbled.

"The dirty dogs!" growled Joe. "They been here and hit it!"

The Kid's grim eyes took in the dead. He could not identify the bodies at sight, for they had been stripped and mutilated. Two bodies bristled like porcupines with arrows, fifty or sixty to each.

"We can't go no farther, Kid," Joe said, slipping from his heaving, lathered horse. "That other gang's comin' back."

"Walls are too hot for us to go inside. . . . Wait! There's a dugout!"

The band of Cheyennes, led by Black Kettle, was almost upon them, yelling in triumph. Bullets whipped into the dirt, or sang in the air about the three scouts as they headed for the scarcely visible dugout near Miller's ruined house.

"Go on, Saber — keep away from them red devils," ordered the Kid, giving his mount a slap on the rump.

The dun understood. He hated the scent of Indians, and was quivering in anger, his merled eye rolling. He flashed between the smoldering ruins of house and barn, and cut away from there.

The other two horses followed him for a short distance but, instead of keeping on, paused to drop their heads and graze. A detachment of Black Kettle's braves circled around to lasso them.

The Rio Kid and his two companions, with their rifles and all the ammunition they had, crawled into the dugout hole. And those three were too experienced to forget their water canteens.

In the Indian country, every ranch had a dugout. A house could be burned over a settler's head, but a dugout could not. Several feet into the earth, a square pit was dug, then a foot-high bank made around the edges. Covered over with boards and sod, and with a small tunnel hole leading underground to it, the dugout could be easily defended.

In this, the Kid and Joe and Mireles, throwing down their belts of bullets, took up their rifles and opened fire through the loop-holes prepared for such a situation.

Their ripping lead threw half a dozen of the charging savages from their horses in as many shots.

"Give it to 'em right!" growled the Kid.

Their roaring rifles spat, their slugs ripping again into the massed savages. Not one of the trio, although he knew what horrible torture awaited him if taken, was anything but cool, and no shots were wasted. In each scout's brain was the memory of what he had just seen; an indelible picture of what could be expected after the Indians had finished with an enemy. But this must be sternly ignored. They *must* be cool now, battling for their own lives. For, trapped in the dugout, they had no chance of escaping.

Ear-drums vibrated with the roars in the confined space. The interior of the dugout was soon sulphurous with acrid powder dust.

Outside, sub-chiefs were shrieking orders, and Black Kettle swerved under the deadly fire of the three whites. The Indians began circling insanely, their favorite maneuver in battle, yelling, riding a ring about the dugout, hanging on by toe and hand, shooting from behind their ponies. But the slugs plugged ineffectually into the thick-packed dirt breastwork of the tiny fort.

"Here comes Black Buffalo and Satanta!" announced Pryor.

"Yeah," replied California Joe. "Reckon they were leadin' the gang that hit here. Half of 'em kept on for their villages, Kid."

"Got prisoners," the Kid said. "I didn't see the boys' bodies."

No one mentioned Sue Miller. The fate of a young white girl, captured by such Indians, was too horrible to let the mind dwell upon it. Pryor earnestly prayed that one of the corpses out there was Sue.

Indian reinforcements came pelting up, and the white scouts knew they would have no chance of slipping out under cover of darkness. The savages would ring them thick as a strangling rope.

But the defenders might hold them off while their ammunition lasted. After that —

The Kid shrugged it off. He had stared death in the face and grinned back too often to weaken now before the Grim Reaper.

At a safe distance, Satanta, Black Kettle and Black Buffalo held a pow-wow.

About the ranch were strewn eight dead or writhing mustangs, and a dozen dead braves, while several wounded were being carried off.

"We give 'em a bellyful of frontal attack, boys," said Bob Pryor, shoving a fresh shell into his carbine breech as he watched through a loop.

California Joe began to sing, with an attempt at nonchalance:

Oh, I left my gal in Kan-sas City,
And say, my frien's, that's a doggone pity!
For I met a young squaw among the
    Sioux,
Who'll carve out my heart if I ain't true.

"Easy on the water, Celestino," warned the Kid. "We may be here awhile."

"Well, at least I can fix this consarned moccasin now," observed Joe. "It's cut the top of my foot all day. . . . Say, Kid, did yuh ever stow away chow at Beefsteak Jake's in Abilene? Why, that's food fit for the gods!"

"Yeah, I was there a couple times, Joe. It's mighty swell grub."

They kept their minds off their own close and vital peril. When the final rush came, the Kid meant to shoot Mireles and then himself, rather than fall into the Dog Soldier's hands.

Joe could suit himself. He knew what it was all about. Many a brave man preferred to die quickly, by his own hand, instead of dying a humiliating torture death as sport for the Indians.

The Kid watched the parley that was going on just outside rifle range. Black Kettle then sang out orders, and about a hundred savages began riding swiftly, just inside range, whooping and shooting at the dugout.

"They're tryin' to draw our fire, boys," said Pryor. "Don't shoot 'less yuh're shore to kill."

The savages were seeking to make them expend their ammunition. Then, when it was gone, the three would be easy prey.

CHAPTER XIII
THE TROOPS RIDE

Hour after hour passed. Black Buffalo and Satanta rode off with some of the warriors, but Black Kettle remained, in command.

The murderous fire that greeted them when they dared come close to the dugout had discouraged even the Dog Soldiers, reckless as they were. It would be better, the chiefs had decided, to let them use their bullets up and then take them.

Through the day, a few half-hearted charges were made but the three scouts drove them back. On the clay floor of the dugout empty shells lay, hardly one having been wasted.

At dark the savages stopped their circling. They slaughtered a beef, one run in off Miller's range, and the scouts, huddled in the dank dugout, chewing on a cracker and with a swallow of water apiece, smelled barbecuing meat, saw the red glow of the Indian fires through the loop-holes.

"Any chance of me gittin' through, Kid?" asked Joe.

The Kid made a survey from all four sides.

"Nope, Joe. They've ringed us. It's light, too, from the fires."

"We better sleep then. One can stand guard. I'll take first whack."

Mireles and Joe curled up in the corners, while the Kid, pistol ready, kept an eye on the foe. Through the night they took turns at such sentinel duty.

At dawn, the Indians resumed the attack. They tried another frontal assault, waves of swift riders shrieking and shooting a hail of lead at the loop-holes, driving up to the very face of the dugout.

Keep 'em goin', boys! bawled the Rio Kid, as they worked their carbines as fast as they could.

Mustangs piled up, getting in the way of following mounts, while the Indians felt the stinging, accurate death lead of the Kid and his companions.

Again they started their circling, forcing the three scouts to expend ammunition. There wasn't much more. The Kid checked up. A few more charges and they must ring down the curtain.

Death was much closer, with no sign of a respite. When the end came, it would come fast. The Kid set his jaw, shrugged his broad shoulders. After all, it had to come some time and it might as well be here as anywhere else.

"Though I do hate to lose out to them sidewinders," he muttered. Besides, his heart was torn for the Millers, for Sue and her people, and he burned for revenge. . . .

Over the vast rolling Kansas plains, a column of troops moved southward. Four hundred wagons, the big blue-bodied, billowing-topped Army vehicles, spread behind the advance guard of Osage scouts.

General George A. Custer, in command in the field of the expedition against the Indian tribes that were laying waste the white settlements of south Kansas, Colorado and northern Texas, had cleverly shortened the flanks of such a long column by running the wagons in four parallel lines so the space that must be protected on the sides was quartered.

The march was toward Indian Territory, where Custer and Sheridan, the latter in command of the military district, had decided to establish a supply base from which to conduct crippling operations against the enemy. Fort Dodge was too far away to the north to strike from.

Captain Louis McLane Hamilton was in command of the advance troop and Major Joel Elliott, Custer's second-in-command had the rear guard, with G, H and M troops.

The Seventh Cavalry troopers were spread out in long lines, on either flank of the wagons, and the Nineteenth Kansas Volunteers, made up of settlers and old soldiers from the Civil War, had been brought along with the crack organization built by Custer.

The Seventh was composed of seasoned men, whipped into shape by Custer, weeded out, trained at marksmanship and soldiering by the great general. Such a job took time. Target shooting, spirit, formation, all had to be drilled into the men who came to the regiment. It was a marvel to see how a good officer could take some rough rascal, bearded and nondescript, who had only enlisted to get in out of the Frontier winter, and metamorphose him into a hard-fleshed, clear-eyed neatly uniformed fighting trooper.

Lieutenant Frank Dixon, recovered enough to ride with the troops, glanced back at the rising dust and felt a swell of pride in the might of the United States, as exemplified by this orderly procession. Dixon's wound had healed quickly, though he still had a pad on the scar. But he had been permitted to take his place in the column. In his new uniform — his old one had been ruined by blood and bullet holes — he looked spick-and-span. He was a bit pale and wan under his bronze, but he felt strong and well. He kept his charger a few paces behind the general, who was chatting with his brother, Tom.

Custer had been kind and understanding with Dixon. His reprimand had been but a warning talk to the young officer concerning the habits of marauding Indians.

Since the wagons were along, each trooper did not have to carry a large pack. These were thrown into the company wagons, marked in black letters on the white canvas. Duffle such as blankets, tents, spare coats, could be transported in the big carriers and the blue-uniformed troopers, encumbered only with arms and clanking sabers, could be ready for instant duty.

At the head of the column rode General Custer, his clear eyes ranging far and wide over the plains. His big staghounds and two smaller dogs ranged on the flanks. As was his custom in the field, the general wore fringed buckskin and a broad Stetson. Special fine revolvers and a hunting-knife were at his waist, and a long-range Springfield breech-loading rifle was in a sling at his long leg.

His buglar rode a few paces behind him, and his general's guidon waved proudly in the breeze. Captain Tom Custer, Benteen, Thompson, and West, Adjutant Cook, and other staff officers formed a group close to the famous general, "Old Curly" to his men, as he was "Pahuska" — "Long Hair" to the Indians. Custer's long yellow curls, his superb physique, magnificent strength, made him a gorgeous picture of military manhood.

General Phil Sheridan had ridden with his military escort to a station on the new railroad where government business had called him. But Sheridan had promised to rejoin them at the supply base to be set up.

Watching General Custer now, and swelling with pride to serve under such a commander, young Lieutenant Dixon's eyes were bright at being allowed to be part of this military display. But other thoughts were also in his mind. He was thinking of Sue Miller, of her sweetness and the softness of her hands when she had nursed him — as he *had* thought, ever since he had told her good-by. And he was thinking of something he vainly tried to shake off — the dread of what her fate might be if the raiding Indians chanced to strike the Miller ranch.

Andy Miller had been delayed at Custer's camp where young Pierce Miller, named after President Franklin Pierce, had enjoyed himself hugely. The Miller herd had finally been paid for when the proper official returned to the camp — thirty-six hours ago — and Andy, with Pierce, had taken his leave of Dixon and his soldier friends, and started for home. With him he carried a note to his sister, from Dixon.

It was a beautiful, crisply cool day near the end of October. No clouds were in the intensely blue sky, and the air was like wine to the spirits of the young soldiers crossing the boundless plains. Buffalo, still counted by the million, prairie dogs, coyotes, antelope and elk, other game, ranged the vast land.

The squad of Osages who rode ahead were splendid in war paint and feathers. Though now serving as guides and scouts to the U.S. Army, they were still barbaric in mind and habits. Romero, or Romeo as everyone called the good-natured breed, was among them as was the chief of the Osages, Little Beaver, who had come to offer his own services and those of a dozen picked scouts to Custer. They had ridden a hundred miles from their village in the Nation to serve the white man against hereditary enemies who had decimated their tribe in countless wars.

Little Beaver turned on his mustang, and called something back, pointing ahead.

Custer immediately took up his field-glasses, and, with his staff trailing him, spurred out to join Little Beaver, who could speak some English.

"Some move — Big Chief see," the Osage chief said. Any officer was a "chief" while the commander was always "Big Chief" to the Indians.

Custer put his glasses to his eyes. It was some time before he could distinguish what Little Beaver had noted with his bare vision.

"It's a horse," he said. "Riderless." Behind them, stretched out for a half mile, plodded the long, teeming military column. Eight hundred men of the Seventh, eleven troops of the Nineteenth Kansas Volunteers, teamsters, officers, troopers, plainsmen and all the array necessary to such an expedition — all blindly following the command of one leader, Custer, magnetic, inspiring, handsome as a blond god.

Custer gave orders. His bugler blew clear, sharp notes. Captain Benteen fell into position at the head of the column. The general himself, with Tom Custer, Hamilton and two other staff officers were to ride ahead with a squadron. A Troop, Dixon's company, was picked, and Dixon rode with them.

The horse which had attracted their attention did not run away. It came trotting closer. Custer watched through his field-glasses. "Saddle on him. It's a dun."

They were a full mile out ahead of the main column when the Osage scouts tried to lasso the dun. However, the animal easily dodged them, and streaked on toward the uniformed officers and troops.

"General!" Dixon exclaimed. "I know that horse! It belongs to the Rio Kid, Cap'n Pryor."

"You're right, Dixon!" Custer agreed. "Bugler — sound a blast!"

The bugle rang out and Saber shook his dark mane and slowed down to a military pace.

"He obeys the bugle calls," Custer remarked. He rode slowly toward the dun, calling to him.

Saber, with his saddle still cinched on his heaving body, lathered and specked with dried mud, eluded Custer's hand, but he circled and came back when the bugle sounded once more.

Custer was worried, and so was Dixon, who heard the general say to his brother:

"Tom, I know that dun. He's a wonderful horse. He carried Pryor through the Civil War and he's as smart as a fox. He'd never leave his master if he could help it. I hope nothing's gone wrong with the Kid, Joe, and that young Mex, Mireles."

"Maybe they're camped near here on their way to report," suggested Tom.

"Possibly. On the other hand, they have been on a very dangerous mission. In my opinion, Pryor must be somewhere near, dead or alive. I'll have to investigate this."

He gave orders, and again bugles rang out in the cool air.

Two more squadrons swung out and with Custer in the lead, they trailed after the skittish Saber. The dun would approach just so near, but was too swift and wary to be lassoed.

CHAPTER XIV
SABER TO THE RESCUE

On and on, the dun led them, breasting wave after wave of the plains. The general direction was southeast, and as the sun began to drop in the western sky, Little Beaver again reported. This time he said he heard firing, guns.

"The Miller ranch isn't far from here, sir," Lieutenant Dixon said, unaware of the eagerness in his voice. For his worry was intensified when the scouts reported shooting ahead.

Saber kept leading them on. At last, the cavalry breasted a final step, splashed across the waters of the creek, and saw before them the ruins of the big ranch.

"There they go!" shouted Custer, drawing his revolver and leading the charge.

The troopers spurred after their commander. Speeding away to the south went Black Kettle and a hundred braves, their swift mustangs flying. They shot back, but the range was long. The eager soldiers sought to overtake them but that was not the sort of fight the savages fancied, and they drew away. However, as soon as the bugles sounded to call back the troopers, and they reluctantly slowed and turned, some of the Dog Soldiers rode back and howled, shooting at them, as though to draw them on southward.

"They want us to follow," Custer said. "So we won't. Anyway, it's useless, for their horses are fresh."

The officers swung in toward the burned ranch. Frank Dixon, appalled, but holding himself in an iron check, rode up and dismounted. Twenty-five carcasses of Indian horses lay about the plain, and perhaps forty or fifty blood spots showed where a savage had fallen, although the Indians had carried off their wounded and dead.

A cheer rang out, almost underfoot. Custer swung, and then they saw the Rio Kid, blackened by dirt and powder-smoke, come crawling out of the dugout. After him came the attenuated California Joe, only his teeth showing light in color, then the Mexican lad, Mireles.

"Good heavens, Pryor!" exclaimed Custer, dismounting and seizing the Kid's hand. "How long have you been in there?"

"Oh, two or three days, Gen'ral," replied Joe. "We was so interested we lost count, didn't we, Kid? Say, have yuh got any real food with yuh, Gen'ral? My belt buckle's rubbed a sore on my backbone!"

The three had surface wounds, scratches and cuts from flying leaden fragments. They were in need of water and nourishment but had come through well.

Dixon was staring at the two awful symbols of Indian ferocity, the corpses in the yard. In the blue far overhead circled half a dozen black specks, vultures.

"Kid," muttered Dixon, fingers vising on Pryor's arm, "Kid, is — is one of them — Sue?"

"Reckon so, Lieutenant."

Pryor still preferred to believe Sue Miller dead, rather than that the Dog Soldiers had carried her off.

There were only the two bodies. Had the little boys been massacred, they could have been quickly identified by their size.

Dixon fought for self-control, nails digging deep into his palms, teeth gritted. He was a soldier and must not show his heartbreak, the emotion that tore him.

The Rio Kid was drinking, long and gratifyingly, from a canteen handed him by Custer himself. It tasted like nectar. And

144

the string of jerked beef on which he began chewing seemed to have the flavor of ambrosia. Mireles and California Joe were wolfing provisions, too.

Pryor suddenly whistled, strains of an old Army song that Dixon had heard in the camps:

Said the big black charger to the little
   white mare,
The sergeant claims yore feed bill
   really ain't fair!

Saber, the dun, came trotting up, nuzzled his master's hand.

"That dun's a marvel!" exclaimed General Custer, patting Saber's arched neck.

The horse bared his teeth, snapping.

"Careful, Saber!" the Kid warned him quickly. "He's the boss! Yuh fool, yuh want to be court-martialed?"

Saber behaved, shivering, rolling his eyes. Custer smiled. He loved animals, and the dun was as clever as a man in his own way.

Any good cavalryman puts his horse above himself, and the Kid was no exception. He began by unsaddling Saber, who had been running around for a couple of days with his leather cinched on. The dun went off to roll after a quick rubdown, and Custer ordered a trooper to have a grain feed ready when Saber returned.

"Lieutenant Dixon," ordered Custer, who had no idea of Dixon's inner emotion at sight of the ravaged ranch, or that the young man had just fully realized how deeply he had fallen in love with Sue Miller, "will you please take charge of a burial detail? If you can identify the remains, do so. You know something about these people — more than the rest of us."

"Yes, sir."

Dixon saluted. There was a white line about his lips, but he was straight as an arrow shaft as he turned to obey.

Troopers found shovels and pick-axes in a small tool shed not entirely burned down.

The two bodies were interred in the Kansas sod.

Dixon came back to report to Custer, who was talking with the Kid in a low voice. The Kid had ridden for him in the Civil War, and was a close personal friend, for Custer, though a famous leader, was not yet thirty, young and vigorous.

"That's splendid, Pryor," Custer was saying with enthusiasm. "Just the information we need for the campaign. Great work!"

"I identified the two bodies, sir," Dixon said.

"Good. Who were they?" asked Custer.

"Benjamin Miller and his wife, General."

The Kid stared at Dixon's face, set in a mask of horror. "Mebbe she got away with the boys, Dixon," Pryor growled.

General George Armstrong Custer was a sensitive and clever man as well as a first-class soldier and genius at military affairs. He had been engrossed in the important information the Rio Kid had given him, and had not noticed Lieutenant Frank Dixon's emotion, which Dixon sought to conceal.

The Rio Kid guessed how Dixon was feeling, however, and one of the reasons for it. A shrewd judge of human hearts, Pryor decided that Dixon had fallen in love with beautiful Sue Miller when she had nursed him after his wounding.

Dixon's eyes were terrible to look at, burning and wide. All the color had drained from under his bronzed skin, giving him a sickly, strange aspect.

Custer frowned as he stared at the lieutenant.

"Lieutenant Dixon, you appear very ill, sir. Perhaps your wound is bothering you. You shouldn't have ridden so soon. When we return to the column, report to Dr. Lippincott for treatment."

"I — I'm all right, sir," choked Dixon, but

he was swaying unsteadily on his feet.

The Kid took his arm.

"Sit down, Dixon." He helped the young officer gently to the log seat on which he and the general had been squatted. To Custer he remarked:

"There was quite a fine family here, suh — Ben Miller's family. He and his wife had three sons, Andy and two shavers, Ollie and Pierce. And a mighty good-lookin' daughter named Sue who sort of nursed the lieutenant when he lay here wounded."

"I met Andy and Pierce," replied Custer. "They only left the column yesterday morning."

"I reckon they're all right," observed the Kid, lying like a man. "Probably the young folks escaped to some neighbor's place."

He winked at Custer behind Dixon's back, and the general understood. He touched Dixon's shoulder.

"We'll no doubt find them safe and sound," he said.

"The Indians have taken her," Dixon said dully. He wiped beads of icy sweat from his brow.

"Brace yourself, Lieutenant," ordered Custer.

He fully comprehended the reason for Dixon's reaction now. Dixon was in love with the Miller girl, and was convinced she had been taken prisoner by the Dog Soldiers.

Little Beaver came galloping up to report. "Big guns, heap lots, Big Chief!" the Osage chief announced. "Better ride heap fast. Too many." He waved to the northwest.

"Sam Lee's ranch is that way," the Kid observed. "He's built a fort there."

"Yes," Dixon agreed. He was fighting hard to control the devastating horror in his heart. "A number of settlers have collected there for defense, sir."

Custer was up on his feet, signaling his bugler. He gave hasty orders, and his fighting men mounted and started after their leader.

Swift riders were despatched to intercept the column and order out reinforcements. The cavalry, led by Custer, with the Rio Kid jogging along on his dun, headed toward the Lee ranch. For over an hour they rode, and the sound of heavy gunfire grew closer.

"Indian smoke signals, Gen'ral," remarked the Kid, pointing directly ahead.

From one of the characteristic isolated buttes that stick up from the plains a long white streamer of smoke showed against the sky; then several short puffs. On that eminence an Indian scout was blanketing and releasing the vapor, telegraphing to his friends in the valley below.

Custer was not the sort to hesitate when the lives of innocent victims were in the balance. He had with him a hundred seasoned fighting men, with plenty of ammunition and courage. He was ready to charge to the rescue when Little Beaver came galloping back, slid his pony to a stop before Custer.

"Many as leaves on tree, Big Chief," he reported.

The soldiers were trotting their horses up behind a shallow, rounded crest that marked the valley of the creek in which Lee's ranch stood. The heavy firing ahead, rolling reports of hundreds of guns, was now echoing close upon them.

A band of fifty braves, Dog Soldiers on swift, trained war ponies, showed over the crest, shouting and gesturing defiance.

They fired on the troopers.

"Tryin' to lead us down there," observed the Kid.

Custer gave his orders, bugles took them up. The troopers dismounted, unhurried, efficient, with carbine and ammunition boxes, six-shooters, sabers, ready for use by each man.

"We'll hold the ridge until the others come up," Custer said.

Advancing at quick pace to the crest, they kneeled, and as the Dog Soldiers retreated ahead of them, they peered down into the valley.

Chapter XV
Lee's Fort

Lee's big ranch was spread on the north bank of the creek, but the timber belt along the stream had been cleared for a quarter of a mile on both sides. The watching soldiers could see the low-lying ranchhouse with its roof smoking where burning arrows had landed, and the corrals, barns, and fences.

The most prominent object, however, was a rude citadel constructed of thick sod bricks and reinforced by a facing of cottonwood logs set like pickets in the earth. A small shelter was roofed in the center of this, in which women and children could be placed, while the fighting force manned the loop-holes.

Terrific gunfire rattled from the tremendous array of Indians who besieged the home-made fort. Bold as brass, sure of their numbers, and signaled by their spies of the size of the approaching cavalry force, the savages continued their assault.

"Why, there's a couple thousand of 'em down there, Gen'ral!" exclaimed the Kid. "Kiowas, Cheyennes, Comanches, Sioux, Arapahoes — yeah, and a few Apaches! Come from that line of villages on the Washita, no doubt!"

The great force of red killers rode their ponies in the favorite circling maneuver around the Lee fort. Puffs of gunsmoke showed from the loop-holes on all four sides of the stockade. The watchers on the heights could make out the squatted figures of the defenders, inside, as they held off the red foe.

Scattered on the flats were thirty or more dead Indian horses, showing the effect of this fire and the accuracy of the frontiersmen with guns. Women were working with their men in the fort, loading spare rifles, bringing up fresh ammunition, tending those wounded by stray bullets that had come through the notches.

"The devils!" growled Custer. "They're determined to slaughter the settlers!"

A large detachment of Dog Soldiers, perhaps two hundred braves, rapidly formed down below. War-bonnets, flamed with dyed eagle feathers from the black heads of Indians, mounted on colorful, bedecked mustangs. The chiefs were shouting orders.

Every brave was painted for war, with barbaric streaks of color on face and arms. Many were completely naked from the waist up, despite the cold.

Apprised of the numbers of the troopers, they impudently charged up at Custer's force.

"Hold your fire, men, until they're close, then aim low," cautioned the general.

He had a fine rifle in his hand, and a .45 in his unbuttoned holster. The Kid had his carbine. Kneeling, the troopers waited for the charge that swept up toward them.

On and on came the Dog Soldiers, reckless and whooping insults, giving a marvelous exhibition of horsemanship. Bullets began whipping over the heads of the soldiers, or sending up spurts of dirt as they plugged into the ground. One man was hit in the ear, but though blood spurted, he did not leave the line, waiting for the order to fire.

"Aim — fire!"

The fierce lines of Indians seemed almost upon them as the carbines roared. Twenty-five savages left their saddles. Others faltered, taking lead, while a dozen more lost their horses, scarcely a hundred yards from the steady soldiers.

The survivors charged on up the slope.

Again they were met by the terrific punishing fire of the trained troopers.

"There they go!" shouted the Kid, leaping up and shooting as fast as he could load.

General Custer was firing his rifle, coolly picking off sub-chiefs, the leaders who were urging their wavering men on. The Dog Soldiers came roaring up. The Kid could see the horrible faces, painted in every color, each one individual — streaks of green, vermilion, black, orange. The wiry Indian mustangs, with bright feathers and lengths of colored ribbons twined in tail and mane, were trained for battle, obeying every slight pressure of the magnificent riders.

But brave and bold as they were, the Dog Soldiers could not keep on into that curtain of lead that wilted their ranks as searing flames kill green leaves. Chief after chief, with glorious bonnets of eagle feathers down their bronzed backs, crashed in the rising dust. The buffalo hide shields, made of several layers of the thickest skin would stop an ordinary bullet, but at this close range, the slugs drove through, killing in spite of "medicine" and shield.

The Dog Soldiers slid to a stop, whipping their mustangs up on hind legs. Those whose horses had been killed under them leaped to the backs of friends' animals, while others bent down to scoop up wounded or dead to carry them off the field.

Several soldiers had felt the bite of Indian bullets. Two men were dead, half a dozen wounded.

"The short-range carbine won't carry to the fort," observed Custer, as they hurried the enemy on with bullets. "I'm going to try with a long-range rifle, Pryor."

The troops ceased shooting as the Indians drew off out of range. Hundreds on hundreds of red men were down on the line of the creek, past the fort, and Custer and several young officers set up powerful guns with which they began peppering the foe down below.

Faintly, on the breeze, they could hear cheers from the besieged in the fort.

"Hamilton, take twenty men and watch the left flank," ordered Custer, between shots.

It was Custer's purpose to engage the large army of Indians, and keep them occupied until his main force came up.

The red men were reloading their weapons, and setting their buffalo-hide shields. Chiefs were exhorting their braves to the fight. The stinging bullets from long-range rifles forced them back on the creek, but they were making ready for a mass charge, their attention diverted from their prey at Lee's.

It was an axiom that to attempt retreat before a superior number of Indians was certain death, and Custer had no idea of falling back. He meant to hold this high ground until his main striking effective arrived on the scene.

"Another hour and we'll engage 'em," he told the Kid.

The general strolled along the line with Pryor, speaking to his men, encouraging them.

"Aim low," he told them again. "And don't waste ammunition."

A tremendous charge was being prepared. This suited the general. Then, as the foe seemed about to begin the mass attack, the Kid heard him mutter an angry exclamation.

"They're breaking!"

Swiftly he gave a command to the bugler. The note, "To Horse," rang out. Then "Prepare to Mount," and "Mount." The stirring charge smote the air, and Custer, his long golden locks flowing in the wind of speed, led the way down the slope straight at the enemy.

But the Indians would not engage. Hundreds on hundreds of savage riders were in pell-mell retreat, splashing through the creek to the south bank and riding madly off toward Indian Territory and the fastnesses of their hidden lairs.

In the distance, the men with Custer could hear the sound of bugles. Then dark lines showed on the sunlit plains.

"Here come the boys, Kid," California Joe remarked, as they rode with the troopers at the running foe.

Diving down into the valley, Custer's hundred troopers sought to slow the Indian rout, but the shrewd red men had full advance information as to the heavy reinforcements coming up. Smoke signals from sharp-eyed watchers had told them. They would not fight trained troops at anything like fair odds. It was not in their strategy.

Custer led his men across the creek, in hot pursuit. But already the Indians were splitting up, spread out like the spokes of a fan, into small bands, to join again at some distant rendezvous. While Saber, and Custer's magnificent charger, Curtis Lee, and other blooded steeds belonging to the Army officers could keep up with and perhaps overtake the swift Indian mustangs, the main body of the troopers were mounted on slower running Army plugs, and were left behind in the rush.

After a time the bugles sounded the halt, and the red-faced, cursing, perspiring soldiers began trotting their mounts back. The Indians were a cloud of dust on the southern horizon.

"The same old story," Custer said bitterly to his brother. "Tom, they won't stand and fight. We've got to catch them when they're immobilized."

The advance of the main force, five hundred troopers led by Major Joel Elliott, Benteen and other Seventh Cavalry officers, appeared at the top of the slope, and came whirling down to join Custer.

Bob Pryor, the Rio Kid, weary from the long fight at Miller's dugout, shoved Saber toward Lee's fort, the gates of which were flung open. Cheering Kansas settlers threw their sweated Stetsons into the air, jumping up and down to welcome the troops who had come up to drive off the great army of Indians.

"She — she might be in there!" someone said at the Kid's elbow, and he swung to see Lieutenant Dixon, who had fought bravely through the engagement, and was now returning from the futile chase after the Indians.

"Yeah, Dixon. By golly, there's Andy Miller! And Pierce!"

Andy Miller came limping out to greet them, a long rifle in one hand. Andy was not more than twenty but he had lived a Frontier life, in all its severity, and such men matured early. A coonskin cap was on his light head, and his blue eyes were somber, his bronzed face as set as an Indian's with stoic fortitude. Pierce, a smaller replica of his older brother, also carried a gun longer than himself. He had been doing duty at a loop-hole.

The Kid and Dixon, from their horses, swiftly looked over the joyous faces of the settlers swarming out to greet Custer. Nearly a hundred had taken refuge at Lee's, come from miles along the line of settlements which had borne the brunt of the terrible Indian raids. These were the pioneers of America, the brave who pushed the line of civilization on in the face of all dangers and hardships.

They were strong faces. Even the women showed they were long-suffering, hardworking, backing up their menfolk. They were of many races, these men and women, and all were of daring strains, having thrown off the ties of the Old World to emigrate to the United States in search of freedom and the land they so fiercely loved. Issuing from the great melting-pot, they were Americans.

The backbone of the nation, as the Rio Kid knew.

Stalwart men and their sons, in buckskin or homespun, some in the blue coats of Civil War days, with a sprinkling of gray showing Confederate veterans, crowded about the soldiers, welcoming them.

"They shore pressed us hard," Sam Lee told General Custer. "I never seen so many Injuns afore."

"They hit us yestidday, at dawn," a bearded rancher explained. "More and more kept comin' up. We seen Satanta and Black Kettle and a bunch of other devils."

Children who had been inside the fort came out, skipping and laughing, eagerly approaching the soldiers, glad to be out of the confined space of the little stronghold.

The Kid pushed through the crush, with Dixon at his heels, to Andy Miller.

"Hey, Andy!"

Young Miller swung from the circle around General Custer.

"Howdy, Kid," he growled.

Dixon, dismounted, seized Miller's arm. Andy winced.

"I got a bullet wound in that one, Dixon. Take the other."

"How about it — where's Sue?" demanded Dixon hoarsely.

The young man's blue eyes were dark as a winter sea. He shrugged dejectedly.

"Yuh been to the ranch?"

"Yes. She — she isn't there. We — found your mother and father."

Andy nodded. His mouth was a straight, hard line.

"Pierce and me got there too late. The house was afire and they'd already kilt Ma and Dad. 'Twas dark, but I could see by the fires burnin'. Indians was thick as fleas round the place. They near got Pierce and me, but our hosses was fresh. We'd had to stop on our way home and hide all day, or we'd've been there when they attacked. I got a bullet in the calf of the leg and another nicked my forearm. Luckily me and Pierce made Lee's 'fore they caught up with us. Bunch of us tried to get over to the ranch but more'n more Dog Soldiers was comin' up and we were druv' back."

"Yuh don't know what happened to Ollie and yore sister then?" growled the Kid.

"Shore I know. The Cheyennes carried 'em both off. If yuh didn't find their bodies at the ranch, that's what happened. I figgered it was that away."

Andy Miller spoke quietly. But he and the Kid and Dixon knew that somewhere in the dark wilderness of the Nation the beautiful girl and the little boy must be prisoners of the Indians, beaten and tortured like other such victims before them, slaves of the squaws.

CHAPTER XVI
CAMP SUPPLY

"General! Help us!"

The Kid, who was done in from what he had been through in the past few days, heard the appeals of the settlers to George Armstrong Custer. Strong men, sturdy women, begged for assistance from the handsome, dashing Indian fighter.

Custer was deeply affected. These Frontier settlers had suffered horribly from the raiding Indian tribes. But he was painfully aware how, back in the settled, safe East, the political squabbles of those who wished to keep control of lucrative Indian agencies and contracts, tied the Army's hands completely.

"The fighting shall be carried to the Indians, and soon," Custer promised. "I guarantee it."

"They need a lesson," growled Sam Lee, his stern face drawn. "They been ridin' high, wide and handsome agin us, Gen'ral, without any real punishment."

"Gen'ral," said Andy Miller, who had shouldered his way to Custer's elbow, "can I go along with yuh?"

Custer stared into Andy's young eyes. He seemed about to shake his head, for his plans were all completed.

"They carried off his sister and little brother, Gen'ral!" someone cried.

"There's a volunteer company you can join, Miller," said Custer. "I'll be glad to have you with me." He pressed the young fellow's hand.

The Rio Kid gave Saber a grain feed, then turned the dun loose to graze and roll. He took his blankets and retired to a haymow in one of Lee's barns. Wrapped warm and snug, he slept.

The sun was again streaming through the cracks in the walls of the square barn when the Kid awoke. He had slept like a log through the whole night, and into the morning. His muscles were stiff, and he had a number of slight wounds where bullet fragments had nicked him. But all in all, he had come through the ordeal well.

Going down the ladder, he stepped out into the crisp fall air. At a big horse trough he washed, then shaved, and cleaned the mud and dust from his clothing.

A company of Custer's troopers were

camped near, and the people of the little fort felt free to wander about. Bearded settlers and their women and small ones were around, hardy folks forced to desert their beloved farms and ranches because of the Indian peril.

"Mornin', Kid," Sam Lee greeted him when, neat as he could make himself, Pryor strolled over to the ranch kitchen to find food.

"Howdy, Lee. Has the gen'ral left?"

"Yeah, he rode on at dawn, to meet his main train. Left a guard here for the time bein'! I hope he catches up with them red devils finally. The country's about ruint."

The Kid filled up gratefully on fried beef broiled over red coals, tin mugs of steaming, fragrant coffee, and raised bread baked by the ranch women. He felt much better when he had eaten, and went out into the sunlight to smoke.

Mireles was already up, and had eaten. He grinned at the Kid.

"Joe, he ride weeth Custair," he informed Pryor.

Dixon and most of the others had returned to the Army column. Tom Custer was in command of the squadron left at the Lee place. Pickets were out, and when a shot and a hail were heard about noon, men sprang quickly to their arms, ready for another fight.

The Kid whistled Saber in, saddled the dun, and rode out toward what seemed to be the center of the excitement, while women and children were hustled inside the fort and the cavalry bugles sounded the alert.

A horse came slowly over the breast of the hill.

"Two men on it, Pryor," remarked Tom Custer, lowering his field-glasses. "One's a trooper — he's supporting another person."

They approached the soldier who was holding up a limp figure in front of him as he rode. He was a picket who had been posted a quarter of a mile out on the hill.

"What is it, Riley?" inquired Tom Custer, as he drew up to the cavalryman with his unconscious burden.

"Sir, I seen somethin' crawlin' along the river bank and fired, thinkin' it was an Injun. I didn't hit him — just warned. He kept crawlin', and restin', crawlin' and restin'. I didn't see any more, so I rode down and found this pore feller. He's bad hurt. Looks like the Injuns had worked on him."

"Bring him in," ordered Tom Custer.

Blood stained the torn white shirt, and the dark pants were ribbons on the man's long legs, with abrasions and bruises visible through the rents. One side of his face was a bloody mess, as though he had been dragged along the ground on it. His neck was limp, head rolling with the motion of the trooper's horse, and his face covered with dried blood and dirt.

They carried him in to the ranch, and laid him out. Hot water was fetched, and the victim washed clean and examined for serious injuries.

"I've seen that feller somewheres before," the Kid thought, hanging around as they took care of the hurt man.

Tall, lean of body, the man lay senseless, eyes shut, while they washed him.

"Got a bullet hole in his side here," Sam Lee announced. "That's the worst of it."

Whiskey was poured down him, and presently he weakly opened his eyes, his face screwed up in pain.

"Where am I?" he whispered. "The Indians, they —"

"Take it easy!" Lee said kindly. "Yuh're safe with us. This is Lee's fort."

"I know that feller!" exclaimed the Kid. "He's the missionary I seen at a tradin' post, in the Nation, teachin' the Injun kids. . . . Howdy, Dobbs. How'd yuh come to run afoul of yore red friends?"

168

Edward Dobbs turned his tortured blue eyes on the Rio Kid.

"Oh — yes, now I remember you, sir. I saw you at the Cheyenne agency."

The Englishman was in a shattered condition from wounds and exhaustion. It was hard for him to talk much. But when he had had another warmed drink, and was covered up after his injuries were dressed, he was able to explain what had happened.

"I rode h'out to visit the village of an h'outlyin' tribe," he told his sympathetic listeners. "H'it — h'it's my work, y' know."

"He's a missionary-teacher," the Kid explained.

"There was smallpox there, I'm sure. Several children were very sick. . . ." He paused for breath, shutting his eyes.

"Take yore time," ordered Lee.

Presently Dobbs resumed:

"H'on my way back to the post I was set h'upon by Cheyennes, who beat me — threatened to kill me. They knew me, too — men who came to the agency — for food. At last I broke h'away — one shot me — in the side — my 'orse ran madly h'off —" Gasping, Dobbs again paused for breath.

It was a familiar tale. The Dog Soldiers, having overtaken their unfortunate victim, who had dedicated his life to helping their

169

children and themselves, had not killed Dobbs. They knew who he was, and considered what they did a fine joke. They had tied the wounded teacher to his horse and then pursued the maddened creature, whooping and firing into the air, until they had tired of the sport.

Driven miles from the agency, Dobbs had lost consciousness. When he had come to, he had managed to work free from the loosely tied ropes. He'd had no idea where he was. Feverish from the wound, he had tried to ride by the sun but had not known which direction the post lay. When night had fallen, he had lost consciousness again, and had awakened to find he was being slowly dragged over the grassy plains as his horse grazed from spot to spot.

Having fallen off during the darkness, one foot had remained caught in the stirrup. When he had finally disengaged himself, the animal had run away. Dobbs had painfully crawled to a creek, bathed and drunk, rested. He had gathered enough strength to walk toward some smoke he saw in the sky, but kept falling down, until finally a picket had sighted him.

"Yuh're lucky to be alive, Mister," growled Sam Lee. "Only reason them Cheyennes didn't torture yuh to death was they knowed yuh so well. Stay here where yuh'll be safe and sound, till yuh're well."

"Thank you," Dobbs replied humbly. "You're very good."

The Kid was eager to rejoin Custer who was headed into Indian Territory to establish a supply base from which he could operate against the enemy. However, the general had left a packet of despatches with his brother Tom, that must be carried to Fort Hays, where General Sheridan had gone. The Kid volunteered to make the dangerous trip, with Mireles as company.

Saddling up, Custer's chief of scouts and his Mexican partner swung into leather for the run to Fort Hays, eighty miles away. . . .

When at last the Kid, having completed his mission, returned to the expedition, he saw the strategic spot where General Custer had set up Camp Supply. It was in the Indian Nation, about one hundred miles south of Fort Dodge.

The four hundred Army wagons had carried the necessary supplies and equipment for this all-important base. Camp Supply was set in the angle formed by the union of Beaver and Wolf Creeks, the two streams joining to become the north branch of the Canadian River.

As the Kid rode down into the spick-and-span big camp, it was gladdening to his military eye. Neat rows of conical Sibley tents, company streets, officers' quarters, the horses, wagons, kitchens, were in precise position. Pickets had challenged the Kid. All was in correct order.

He headed for Custer's tent. The general's standard and a sentry were posted outside, and Custer's big staghounds lay as close to their master's quarters as they could get.

California Joe, lounging with some soldiers about the warmth of a fire, smoking his ever-present briar pipe, sang out:

"Hey, Kid, how's the gals at Fort Hays?"

"Fine," answered Pryor. "All lookin' for you, Joe — with shotguns!"

The troopers laughed, and Joe winked.

"It's a fact, boys," he said. "I'm a lot safer among Injuns than with women. They're always pesterin' me."

Custer was in his tent, where a small stove kept the worst chill off.

"Glad to see you back, Pryor," he said, shaking hands. "What news?"

The scout handed his return despatches to Custer.

"Gen'ral Sheridan's on his way here, sir. He'll make it in a couple days."

"Thanks, Captain. Now — how far would you say we are from Black Kettle's winter

172

village on the Washita?"

"Gen'ral, I could ride it in a couple days, mebbe less. But it'll take four or five, reg'lar marchin'. 'Course there's no chance of surprisin' 'em if we march near durin' the daytime."

"That's about what I figured. Keep this under your hat, Pryor, but when Sheridan arrives, I mean to start. Everything's ready."

"Good! The quicker them Dog Soldiers learn the Army can reach 'em and hit 'em hard, the sooner Kansas and the Frontier'll be safe."

The Kid saluted, and went out into the crisp air.

Chapter XVII
The Spy

Custer had eight hundred men of his own regiment, and around five hundred of the Nineteenth Kansas Volunteers with him at Camp Supply. He had, as well, about forty special sharpshooters organized into a company under Colonel West, a veteran Indian fighter.

There was always work around a military encampment. The horses had to be grazed and groomed, clothing washed, wood collected, food prepared. There were roll-call and target practice, and the Seventh Cavalry regimental band, which Custer took with him even into battle, had its practicing to do.

The Kid, having finished his official business, joined Mireles at a company kitchen, where they received a handout of hot food and coffee, gratifying after the cold meals they had eaten on the way back from Fort Hays.

"Reckon I'll have a few winks," the Kid told Celestino, for they had done most of their riding at night, the usual procedure through Indian country.

He retired to a tent and, wrapped in blankets and with a buffalo robe for a couch, he slept. . . .

It was dark when he awoke although taps had not yet sounded, and the red glow of the big fires showed on the tent walls and through the slits where the canvas did not overlap.

The Kid yawned, cozy and snug in his blankets, the warmth of the buffalo hide keeping the penetrating cold from creeping under him. He had relaxed entirely in the security of the Army camp, for alert pickets covered all approaches and military police were in charge of the various company grounds.

In the dim light he could see Celestino, the Mexican's long form stretched under his covers on the other side of the tent. He could hear soldiers talking in their snug tents, warmed by wood fires.

Pryor was lying with his feet toward the front of the Sibley, where canvas strings held the two sections together. He closed his eyes again, lulled by the familiar sounds of the Army camp. He had almost drowsed off

175

again when a soft sound roused his curiosity, and he again became alert, listening. The noise was difficult to identify, and he thought it was close to his head.

Turning his eyes back without shifting his body, he saw something bright glint as it slowly moved up the wall of the tent. In the dimness he did not at once realize what it was.

However, as a black line followed the path of the shining thing, he suddenly recognized the blade of a long knife, cutting a slit in the back of the tent.

"Well, dang my hide," he thought, waiting, feigning sleep. "Mebbe Joe's playin' one of his tricks on me!"

A mittened hand parted the canvas and a man's head and shoulders came through without a sound that might waken a sleeper.

It wasn't California Joe, but a man in Army blue. He had left off his overcoat, but the Kid could see his tunic and brass buttons, the fatigue cap on his head. The fellow wore no beard or mustache, and the Rio Kid couldn't recognize the vague blur of his face as he quietly came inside and crouched at the rear.

Thinking he had a sneak thief to deal with, Pryor waited, watching him through lowered lashes.

The night marauder squatted in the faintly lit tent, letting his eyes grow accustomed to the change from the firelight outside. In his right hand he still gripped the long knife, its twelve-inch, savage blade a weapon of the first magnitude in a skilled man's hold.

He was looking straight at the Kid, his teeth gritted together. He shifted, slowly, and raised the long-knife, throwing himself in to drive the point into the Kid's exposed eye and hit his brain for a quick, silent kill.

Taken by surprise as he swiftly realized that this man was not a camp thief, the Rio Kid rolled away. His body struck the taut side of the tent, pegged down to the frozen ground, and as the knife drove into the blankets and buffalo robe, where he had lain just a second before, he was pushed back against the man's lowered arm by the reaction of the tight cloth.

"What the devil!" snapped the Kid, hurriedly working his hands out as the marauder, off balance from his miss, recoiled, trying to disentangle the knife from the folds of the Kid's covers.

Pryor heard the startled hiss of the fellow's breath, and a big gloved fist struck him in the nose. It felt like a sledgehammer, and brought smarting water to Pryor's eyes.

Bringing up his legs, he kicked at his

antagonist, thus parrying the second stroke of the knife. The sharp blade would have cut his legs seriously had not the blankets and buffalo hide taken the slice.

His swift kick sent the burly fellow back against the tent, just as Mireles awakened.

"What ees?" the startled youth cried, throwing off his blankets, coming to his knees.

The Kid's gun was close at hand, but he was tangled up in the covers, trying to get his body clear. With a hoarse curse, the killer threw himself back, and was through the slit he had made before the two could seize him.

In a flash, Pryor set up a cry:

"Stop thief! Sentry!"

He buckled on his gun as he plunged through the gap left by the would-be knifer.

"There he goes, Celestino!"

He saw the running figure at the end of the company street, ducking around a row of tents out of sight, and dashed at full-speed to overtake him. Answering shouts came from alert pickets. Officers, seizing their weapons, emerged from their tents, believing an Indian attack might be imminent.

The Kid galloped after the marauder, swung the turn and fell into the arms of a street sentry.

"Hey, what's goin' on?" demanded the sentry, one of Custer's Seventh Cavalry troopers. "Yuh been drinkin'?"

"No — but one of yore men just tried to drive a knife into me while I slept!" shouted the Kid. "Let go, soldier! Which way'd he go?"

"Who?"

"Didn't yuh see anybody come through this aisle?"

"Seen one of them volunteers a minute ago, that's all."

General Custer came rapidly along the company street, a revolver in one hand.

"What's wrong, Pryor?" he asked.

"Sir, someone just tried to kill me," the Kid replied. "He went over there among the volunteers."

General Custer took the lead, followed by other officers, the Kid and a squad of troopers.

But on the ground where the Nineteenth Kansas Volunteers camped, the few soldiers outside their tents had not recognized the man who had tried to kill Pryor.

He had managed to reach a tent, and slip inside.

"Turn out your men, Captain," snapped Custer. "At once. Line 'em up."

The bugles trilled the command. Troopers came pouring from their tents, rapidly lining up. Fresh fuel was thrown on the fires, sending them leaping to the sky and giving a bright illumination as Custer and the Kid, trailed by the general's staff, started down the rows of soldiers.

The Kid stared into each face, seeking to identify his assailant. He hoped he could recognize the fellow one way or another.

About halfway down one row, he found a man whose face was red, and who, as the Kid watched, was unable to conceal the fact that he was breathless.

"Step out!" growled the Kid.

Closely he scrutinized the soldier's features. "Gen'ral!" he cried suddenly. "I'm shore that's the man! His name's Horseface Keyes and he works for Indian Agent Vandon! Shaved off yore mustache and beard, but I know yuh, Keyes!"

The red in Keyes' cheeks heightened.

"Keyes is a spy, Gen'ral Custer," the Kid went on quickly. "I told yuh Vandon's in cahoots with Black Kettle, Satanta and Black Buffalo, supplyin' 'em with guns and likker. A hundred to one Keyes is here to keep Vandon informed of our movements! I'm a dangerous witness against 'em and Keyes tried to put me outa the way!"

180

"Sergeant — arrest that man!" ordered Custer.

Keyes had no chance to run, surrounded by soldiers. Cursing, protesting, he was seized by the military guard, and his rifle and revolver taken from him.

"Search his tent," snapped Custer.

A long knife was found under Keyes' blankets. Caught in the hilt was a tiny thread of canvas.

Brought at Custer's command to the general's tent, Keyes was stood up while Custer and the Kid interrogated the spy.

"Do you realize, Keyes," Custer said severely, "that this is a most serious matter? We are at war, and the penalty for a spy at such a time is death."

Keyes scowled. He assumed an air of bravado, but would not talk.

"If you wish to help me, Keyes, I might commute your sentence to imprisonment instead of a firing squad," Custer urged. "Vandon, according to my information, is abetting the hostile Indians against the United States."

"Vandon sent Keyes here after me, no doubt of it, Gen'ral," insisted Pryor. "He's watchin' yore movements, too."

"Yuh lie!" snarled Keyes. "I joined up with the Volunteers a few days back to get even

181

agin the Injuns! They kilt my brother."

"That doesn't explain why you tried to murder Captain Pryor," Custer said coldly.

Keyes shrugged. His eyes sought the lantern, burning on the rough table, with Custer's maps and papers spread out on the top.

"Now what's he plannin'," the Kid thought, keeping a close watch on the big prisoner.

Chapter XVIII
Winter Campaign

Keyes showed the Kid what he was planning, an instant later. It came, the desperate, last-chance attempt of the trapped spy and killer to escape. With his left arm, Keyes swept the lantern from the table while from inside his blue tunic he whipped a snubnosed, double-barreled derringer of large caliber.

Custer was quick as a tiger. He was nearer Keyes than the Kid and lunged to seize the desperate man's rising arm. Keyes was more afraid of Pryor, whom he had seen in action, than he was of the general. He had meant to kill the Kid first, but Custer's play sent him reeling back, the derringer swinging on the general. The little gun was deadly at such close range.

Oil from the lantern was burning on the floor, the smell of the hot glass and kerosene filling the tent; the red glow from the fires outside lighted the walls of the tent.

The Rio Kid acted with the speed of a light streak, his hand that flew to his Colt a blur. Pryor's .45 roared, seemed joined to Keyes' lighter-throated gun explosion.

The general felt the wind of the first bullet from the derringer, and the Kid's did not come far from him, but Pryor knew it was life or death, and was forced to take the chance.

In the uncertain light, Keyes could be seen, staggering back. Between his eyes was a token from the Rio Kid — a bullet-hole. An instant-fraction later, the Kid's follow-up hit him in the side and whipped him around. He crashed at Custer's booted feet.

It was over, the desperate play for freedom staged by Horseface Keyes. He had meant to shoot them both down, break out the rear of the tent, seize a horse and escape in the night.

"Autie, what's up?"

Tom Custer sprang inside, his face anxious, for he feared his brother had been hurt.

General Custer was staring at the fallen Keyes. He looked back, at the Rio Kid.

"Good shooting, Captain," he said simply.

As soon as the excitement died off, the men returned to their snug blanket rolls and tents, for it was bleak and cold. . . .

The following afternoon, General Sheridan and staff arrived at Camp Supply. This was all that Custer was waiting for. He had picked his cavalry, and the best teams and wagons to transport rations and fodder for between eight and nine hundred seasoned troopers. The rest would remain to guard Camp Supply.

Andy Miller, yearning to find his missing sister, Sue, and his little brother, Ollie, was in the scouting division that was presided over by the Rio Kid and California Joe. Pryor had become great friends with Little Beaver and Hard Rope, the Osage chiefs. Both Indians were a valuable addition to the force with which Custer and Sheridan hoped to end the reign of blood on the Kansas Frontier.

On the evening of November twenty-second, General Custer called his staff together. Sheridan, though he was Custer's superior, had ordered that he was to be considered as an observer and that Custer was to have full charge of field operations.

The Rio Kid, sitting in the background, listened to the famous Indian fighter's orders.

"Gentlemen," General Custer said, "tomorrow we start, promptly at daybreak, to strike at the villages on the lower Washita."

"What about this snow, General?" asked the adjutant anxiously.

"Just what we want," replied Custer.

Big flakes had started to fall that afternoon, and the sky was a dark, leaden hue.

"We can move, but the Indians can't," reminded the general.

The Rio Kid was glad that at last they were to go into decisive action against the red killers of the plains. He had made all necessary preparations for the expedition, for which he would scout, with the Osages and California Joe breaking trail well out in advance of the first troops.

In the morning, the Kid woke to the clear notes of reveille. It was still snowing, and an icy wind cut the valley, flapping the canvas tents. He quickly pulled on his overcoat and heavy boots, checked his guns and carbine, and started out, with Mireles at his heels.

"B-r-r!" Mireles shivered. The Mexican hated the cold, but would follow his friend anywhere in the world and back.

A foot of snow lay over the camp ground and surrounding country, transforming it into a white wilderness from which stuck out bare cottonwood limbs. The snow came almost to the top of the Kid's high boots as he waded through to the kitchen, where a fire was going. The horses were shivering, as they waited. Troopers stood around, drinking hot coffee, up to their knees in the snow.

It was not yet full daylight, but a grayish dull hour. The bugle blew, and the Kid, grooming Saber lovingly despite his half-frozen hands, saw the men stirring quickly as they took down tents and packed wagons for the march. Soon the troop commanders reported all ready save for saddling.

"Boots and Saddles" came. The soldier lived by bugle calls.

Each trooper grasped his saddle and slapped it on his mount's back, tightening girths and other straps.

General Sheridan was to remain here. He stood in his tent door, and Custer pushed his charger over to say good-by.

"Good-by, old fellow," Sheridan cried. "Take care of yourself!"

"To Horse" was sounded, and each trooper stood at his horse's head. Then the commands blew — "Prepare to Mount," and "Mount."

The column was ready to march. Up front the Kid sat his Army-trained dun, in command of the scouts, red and white. His partners, Mireles and California Joe, were close at hand.

Custer, flanked by his great staghounds, and his staff officers, Tom Custer, Captain

Louis Hamilton, Colonel Cook, Captain Benteen, and Major Elliott, led the regiment. The band was in front of the first troop, where Lieutenant Frank Dixon rode the flank with his men.

"Advance!"

At this bugle call, the band struck up the famous marching song, "The Girl I Left Behind Me," and the column started to roll out of Camp Supply.

It was hard going for Saber, carrying the Kid through the snow, and visibility was poor. However, like all Army officers, the Kid carried a good compass and could lay out a course by this.

The storm raged on, as the horses, heads down to it, broke through the snow. About two P. M., the Kid and Little Beaver, the Osage chief, hit the valley of Wolf Creek, where there was plenty of timber, and picked a camping spot. They had come fifteen miles through the blizzard. While waiting for the wagons to come up, every man started to gather wood. All were in good humor despite the weather and hard going.

Soon fires were blazing high on the different company grounds, and as the wagons pulled in, food and hot drinks were made ready. Tents were pitched, and fires built inside them. . . .

At four o'clock the next morning, the Kid sprang from his buffalo robe and blankets, and California Joe grunted, rising up.

"Snow's stopped, Joe," Pryor cried.

"Fine goin' — overhead," growled Joe.

After a quick breakfast, the Kid mounted and led the way toward the Antelope Hills, where Custer, on his scouts' advice, had determined to strike the Canadian.

A column of troops moved far slower than the swift scouts could alone, and besides they were hampered by the deep snow. It took three days of marching before they sighted the Antelope Hills, and the Kid led them into camp on the north bank of the Canadian.

Here a ford had to be found that would take the wagons, and California Joe and the Kid began searching for one. Joe glanced ahead, to where loomed the towering battlements of the Antelopes.

"Say, Kid, yuh ride down thataway," he said. "I'll go this."

"Better stay together, hadn't we, Joe?"

"Nope. I'll meet yuh at camp, Kid."

Pryor didn't argue. Joe seemed eager to be rid of him, so he swung right up the torturous winding red course of the river.

"Now what's he got under his hat?" the

Kid said to his dun.

Curious, the Kid pushed through the snow to a thicket on a hillside. The high point gave him a view of the lower section where Joe had ridden. He was rather surprised to see that the lean scout had left his horse on the bank and was standing shin-deep in the water, ice-cold as it was.

"Mebbe testin' for quicksand," he thought.

Joe worked along near the bank, stooping to feel around in the water. At the distance, the Kid could not make out what it was that interested Joe so greatly that he would stand and stare at his hand for minutes.

Then the Kid suddenly remembered the glint of yellow and silver metals that Joe and he had observed when they had come through here on their way back to Custer. He slapped his leathered thigh and chuckled.

"So that's what the old coot's so sly about — shakin' me," he muttered. Joe always had been an inveterate placer miner, when he was not scouting.

At last Bob Pryor discovered a place where laden wagons might cross the treacherous bed of the river, and rode back to Custer to report. California Joe, damp and chilled, came in an hour later, but said nothing to Pryor about what he had been doing.

The horizon was a great circle of snowy whiteness. One by one the huge Army wagons, with their immense white covers, started across the river and ascended the slopes from the valley. The Kid, out ahead with his Osages, suddenly came upon fresh tracks, plainly visible in the snow. After checking, he returned to tell Custer.

"A couple of hundred hostiles, General," he reported. "Tracks ain't twenty-four hours old. They cut down from Kansas when the storm started and are headin' toward the big villages on the Washita."

Custer summoned his bugler, gave his orders. Quickly his staff assembled.

"We leave the wagons here, gentlemen," he said. "Each man will pack only what can be strapped to his saddle. Make sure cartridge boxes are filled. The train will follow us as it can. One hundred rounds of ammunition per man, coffee and hard bread, and a small allowance of fodder will be taken. Tents and extra blankets remain with the wagons. Light marching order."

He swung, saying:

"Captain Hamilton, you are officer of the day. I'll leave eighty men with you, and you must push after us as rapidly as the teams can move."

The Rio Kid, with a cigarette twirling blue smoke from his lips, saw Hamilton's face fall. To a soldier of such ambition, to be left with the wagons was heartbreaking. His squadron was one of the finest in the command.

Custer knew this, but it was Hamilton's hard luck to be officer of the day and he must remain. The Kid watched the byplay, inwardly amused, although he was fully in sympathy with young Hamilton. After awhile, Hamilton came riding up to Custer, who was busy superintending the preparations.

"Sorry, Captain," Custer said. "If you could find an officer who doesn't feel up to the hard trip ahead —"

"General, I have done that," Hamilton cried eagerly. "He's Johnson. He's snow-blind and half-ill."

"Very well, then."

"Shall I join my squadron?"

Custer nodded, smiled. He liked such spirit in his officers.

The advance was sounded. The Kid, Joe and the Osages, out ahead, followed the Indian trail like bloodhounds. The weather had moderated somewhat, and all through the day they kept rapidly on.

It was after dark when the command

halted, for coffee and a quick meal. Horses were unsaddled, unbitted and given a feed of oats and a drink, while fires could be lighted under protection of the steep creek banks.

"Moon'll be well up in an hour, Gen'ral," the Kid said to Custer. "That war party ain't so far ahead of us."

"We start again at ten," replied Custer.

"Good. Night ridin'll be safer. We can come up on 'em without bein' spied."

CHAPTER XIX
BATTLE OF THE WASHITA

Just three or four hundreds of yards out in advance, the Rio Kid and the Osage scouts smelled out the trail. Back among the troops silence prevailed, no talk or unnecessary sound permitted. The men were forbidden to so much as strike a match.

It was eerie, riding in the silver, still moonlight, with only the soft crunch of snow under the shod hoofs of the hundreds of cavalry horses to break the silence. Stark tortured shapes of bare trees stuck up against the night sky.

After a time, the Kid swung the dun, rode back to Custer.

"Little Beaver smells smoke, Gen'ral!" he informed. "And I know we're close to the spot where I saw the big villages."

The Osage scouts were on foot, now, nearing the crest of a hill, to creep up and peer cautiously over its top. After their reconnaissance, Little Beaver came stealthily to the Kid and the general.

"Heap Injuns down there," he grunted.

Dismounting, the Kid and Custer followed Little Beaver to the hill crest.

"That's the place!" the Kid whispered. "Their horses are down below!"

In the distance, they heard dogs barking. Then a small bell tinkled, a bell hanging round the neck of the mustang herd leader.

It was just past midnight — and the great moment for which all this long preparation had been made was fast approaching!

Dawn was the hour set for attack. Before that Custer must get his men into position. After making sure that all was quiet in the big Cheyenne village below, the Kid returned with the general.

Custer was in command of about eight hundred mounted troopers, picked men. He split them into four groups.

Major Elliott, commanding Troops G, H and M, moved from Custer's left so as to circle to the rear of the village and cut off the retreat of the Indians. The other three groups were sent in three other directions. It was imperative to attack such a camp from all sides or the elusive redskins would slip away.

Colonel Thompson, with B and F troops, moved to the right so as to connect with

Elliott. Colonel Myers, commanding E and I troops, moved to position a mile to Custer's right. A, C, D and K troops, forty sharpshooters led by Colonel Cook, the Osages and white scouts — among them the Kid — were with Custer himself.

Captain Hamilton, who commanded one of these squadrons, and Lieutenant Frank Dixon eagerly awaited the moment for the attack. Andy Miller, squatted on the snow, his rifle across his knees, grimly prepared for revenge upon those who had kidnaped his beloved sister and brother. The Kid knew how these two felt, and knew how they were hoping against hope to find Sue Miller in the Cheyenne village, alive, although it was Indian custom to kill their prisoners at the instant of attack.

No fires could be permitted as the cold vigil began. Even the crushing of snow under tramping, stamping feet made too much noise so the half-frozen troopers were compelled to wait in silence. In the terrible cold of the winter night the weary men sat or stood on the snow beside their horses.

The Kid lounged with his scouts. California Joe was talking as usual, in a low voice, telling his interminable stories. The Osages silently listened. The heavy-set, thick-lipped Romeo sat at the Kid's left.

"Do you think they'll fight, Joe?" Custer asked, as he paused by their group.

"Fight!" replied Joe. "I got nary a doubt as to that, Gen'ral. There's a couple thousand Injuns down there in that village and the Kid says there's more along the Washita. We got to get the bulge on 'em."

The hours seemed interminable before the east began to glow perceptibly lighter, and then came the command to get ready. Every man of these eight hundred cavalrymen with Custer knew they must win or they would be wiped out.

"Do not shoot until the signal is given," Custer ordered. "Keep cool, men, aim low and don't waste ammunition."

The band, mounted, had their instruments ready. The leader kept his cornet at his lips, as Custer led the advance on the village in the valley of the Washita.

Soon they were near enough to see the tall white lodges, standing in irregular lines among the trees, with faint smoke columns issuing from some where fires had been kept going all night.

Dead silence. Then a single rifle shot rang out on the far side of the village. General Custer swung around to the band leader, made a gesture with his hand.

" 'Garry Owen,' " he directed.

The rollicking notes of the regiment's fighting tune burst on the cold air, filling the valley. Loud cheers rang from the throats of the troopers. Bugles sounded the charge, and fighting men dashed full-tilt at the Indian village.

The Rio Kid was among the first to reach the tents. He had left off his overcoat so he might fight with more freedom. His six-guns loaded and ready in their holsters, and his short-barreled carbine was in his hand.

The music of the band, the blaring of the bugles, the yells, roused the Indians, caught napping by the surprise attack over the snow. But they were instantly running from their tepees, rifles, bows and arrows in hand, springing behind trees for defense. A number of them made the bank of the Washita, behind which they took cover and began firing at the charging troopers who were swarming into the village from every direction.

The sharp crack of hundreds of Indian rifles tore the air, answered by the heavy-throated carbines of the troops.

The Rio Kid, tearing along the line of tepees, shooting down braves who with rifles and bows drove death at their foes, was fighting promiscuously, dashing this way and that.

Suddenly a big savage darted from a tepee, a heavy rifle up. It blared, and Captain Louis Hamilton, a few yards away on his horse in advance of his squadron, took the bullet in his heart and crashed to the ground, a terrible gaping wound pumping the dashing young officer's heart-blood from his body.

With a wild war-whoop, the Indian chief swung on the Kid, who swerved the dun and fired point-blank into the redman's face. In that swift flash, the Kid recognized Black Kettle, chief of all the Cheyennes. But he was chief no longer, for Black Kettle flipped back, gun flying from his powerful grip, dead before he sprawled in the snow.

Indians were falling throughout the village. The crashes and flashes of hundreds on hundreds of guns made the new dawn hideous, mingling with the hoarse cries of soldiers, the shrill war-whoops of the Cheyennes. All was blood and confusion. Squaws and young ones were running for the woods, many of the Indian women shooting revolvers at the troopers as they retreated. Groups of fighting warriors took what cover they could, and a hundred single fights merged into one great battle.

Lieutenant Dixon, with Andy Miller at his side, slid up to the Rio Kid.

"Have you seen her, Kid?" gasped Dixon.

He gripped a smoking six-shooter in one hand, and Miller's rifle was hot, for the two had been raging through the village, hunting Sue as they fought.

"Nope!" the Kid said soberly. "Black Kettle's dead, though. C'mon! We got to keep on fightin'!"

He swung onto his dun and flashed off, shooting into the battling savages. He passed General Custer who was dismounted and using a rifle, while Tom Custer stood near his brother. Both the famous officers were in the hottest part of the scrap as they always were. But just as the Kid passed them, Tom Custer was whipped around as though by a giant hand, and clutched at his heart. His brother caught him as he fell.

"We're losin' good men," the Kid growled grimly. "Hamilton, and now Tom!"

That added to his battle fury, which rose to fever pitch. Clouds of powder-smoke drifted up over the Cheyenne village. Screams and shouts mingled with the gunfire in terrific volume.

The crying of a child, however, reached the Rio Kid's keen ears from close at hand. He swerved around a big tepee, mantled with snow, and saw that the back had been pushed up. A squaw was emerging, dragging a small figure by one arm.

"Lemme go, dang yuh, yuh red devil!"

"Ollie!" cried the Kid. "Ollie Miller!"

A huge Cheyenne Dog Soldier, who had been firing from his tepee at the soldiers, leaped from the gap. He leveled a carbine at the Kid, who instantly threw himself from his saddle. The Indian's first slug bit a chunk from his Stetson, but the Kid fired on the breath of his foe's shot. The Dog Soldier crashed back and slid down the hide wall, twitching in the snow.

The squaw, seeing her young prisoner was about to be rescued, raised a knife to plunge it into Ollie's heart. Pryor lunged for her, knocking her back, and snatched Ollie.

"Where's yore sister?" he demanded. "She in that tepee?" He feared they might have salughtered Sue at the moment of attack.

"I ain't seen her," gasped Ollie.

The little boy's face was covered with dirt, his hair awry. He wore scraps of hide for clothing and in the gray light of dawn looked much like an Indian child. He was covered with bruises and cuts. However, he had no serious wounds.

The Kid lifted him to the dun's back, and rode rapidly off, seeking a place of safety for the boy. He sighted Dixon and Andy as they emerged from a tepee in front of which lay a couple of dead braves.

"Hi, Dixon!" he called. "I got Ollie!"

Andy Miller cried out in joy, as he rushed to his little brother, hugged him and sheltered him in his arms.

"Sue — where is she, Ollie?" he choked.

Dixon's face was a set mask, stern in the rising light of the new day.

"We've hunted every tepee in the village," he growled.

Ollie began to weep.

"Brace up," the Kid said, patting him. "Yuh're safe now."

"I ain't seen Sis, I tell yuh," sobbed Ollie. "Not since the night they 'tacked the ranch, Andy. She run out and tried to get a hoss to fetch help, but they got her."

"She's dead, then?" asked Andy.

"Reckon so, if yuh ain't found her by this time. Most likely they shot her or mebbe some of the other Injuns captured her."

The Kid turned the dun, and returned to the fight. The Indians had fled from the village, and were endeavoring to rally at various points, shooting and firing arrows in swarms. Though outnumbered nearly three to one, the trained troopers of General George A. Custer had, by the surprise attack, routed the enemy and cut them off from their large horse herds.

Little Beaver streaked past Pryor, a blood-dripping scalp raised in one hand, a long knife in the other. He grinned as the Kid hailed him. In his barbaric mind he had helped settle the score for the Osages.

The battle spread over a large area. Gunfire was heavy, and wounded and dead lay on the field, stricken warriors from both sides. And into the thick of it charged the Rio Kid, on his battlewise mount.

Saber loved the scent of burnt powder, the din of battle. The dun would rush in to attack, nostrils flared, merled eye rolling, teeth bared as he carried his hard-fighting master into the fray. Bullets drove around the Kid. Several touched him but he did not catch one with his name written on it.

The bugles were blaring, while the band, on a little rise, kept playing "Garry Owen" at full blast. Finally the troopers, obeying the bugles, dismounted and began to close ranks. The mounted charge was over and the rest of the battle was to be on foot. Bob Pryor, of course, not being subject to military discipline, as a scout, stuck to his saddle, heading for points where resistance seemed strongest.

As the hours passed, the contest raged on. The Indians were driven from every point, leaving dead and wounded on the field. The

Kid, pausing to reload his hot guns, looked to the summits of the hills surrounding the valley of the Washita.

"They're comin' thick and fast!" he muttered, and went to find General Custer.

The general was in the hottest part of it, as usual. California Joe had just come in, to report that he and his men had captured nearly a thousand Indian ponies.

Custer swung, staring at the groups of savages on the hills who, from a safe distance, were watching the battle in the valley.

"Aren't they Cheyennes who've escaped?" he asked.

"I don't think so, Gen'ral," the Kid replied. "We've got the Cheyennes purty well smashed, I'd say. I b'lieve they're from the other villages I saw."

"Well, go and check up," ordered Custer. "Take Mireles with you and as many men as you need!"

Chapter XX
The Kid Takes a Prisoner

Quickly the Kid picked up Celestino, who was lying on a flat rock, firing a sharpshooter's rifle at the foe. Little Beaver, too, was willing to leave his plunder and enemy scalps, and ride with the Kid. They plunged into the woods, where dismounted cavalrymen, carbines in hand, were cleaning up squadrons of Indians, making prisoners or fighting it out with those who refused to surrender.

The Kid and his two companion scouts rode cautiously. A half mile from the village the din of the main battle grew less. They crossed a feeder brook, and swung up the wooded slope.

Suddenly the dun snorted, laid back his ears and shivered.

"What's up, Saber?" muttered the Kid.

Then, out on a level, snow-covered stretch, he saw the dead.

The three scouts stared in silence at the

awful sight. Naked, mutilated bodies lay in a circle — Major Elliott and his little party. And the signs showed how desperate had been the struggle they had put up. These men must have been taken by surprise and suddenly surrounded by a large band of Indians, perhaps a hundred to one, but they had sold their lives as dearly as possible, as attested by many blood spots in the snow.

The Kid, eyes dark, picked up the trail of the savages who had committed the deed. With Little Beaver and Mireles, the scout rode on, alert and ready.

"I smell 'um, Chief," Little Beaver grunted suddenly.

The dun, too, was sniffing the air with distaste, hating the scent of Indians as he did.

The Kid dismounted and, with Little Beaver, crept through the thickets, white with snow.

"Satanta!" he breathed, as he saw his arch-enemy, the giant Kiowa chief. Satanta sat a handsome paint pony and his face was streaked with war paint. He was alone, though two sub-chiefs could be seen farther up the hill. No doubt Satanta had dropped behind his main party. Perhaps he had caught some slight sound of the Kid's approach, though the wind was in Pryor's favor.

"Sneak back and fetch me my lariat, Little Beaver," ordered the Kid, using sign language.

Little Beaver crept away, noiselessly, and the Kid held a bead on Satanta, determined to kill the chief if he started off. But the Kiowa didn't move before Little Beaver returned, thrusting the rope into the Kid's hands. Pryor preferred making a prisoner of the important chieftain, rather than to shoot him.

In sign talk the Kid indicated that Little Beaver was to take care of the other two Kiowas while he concentrated on Satanta. He coiled his noose and made ready to cast. Then the oiled lariat whipped out, fell over the astounded Satanta's head.

The Kid jerked with all his might. The noose around his arms prevented Satanta from getting up his weapons. The skittish paint pony leaped madly, and even Satanta's iron knees could not hold, with the rope pulling him. He crashed, floundering in the snow, sliding with the Rio Kid's yanks. The blanket he had cast over his shoulders slipped off, showing the major-general's tunic Custer had given him.

Satanta's two sub-chiefs swung, and with

wild war-whoops spurted to his aid. Little Beaver downed one before the brave was fairly started, and a moment later hit the horse of the other one. The rider, lithe as tempered steel, landed on his feet and began running, but Little Beaver got him in the ribs. He flew through the air, dead before he landed, splotching the snow with crimson.

"Help me!" ordered Pryor.

Swiftly Celestino and Little Beaver rushed upon the great Kiowa chieftain, making him helpless with coils of rope. Covered with snow, trussed, Satanta glared at them with his fierce, dark eyes.

War-whoops came from above. The Kiowas up there were preparing to ride down and assist their chief.

"It must have been the Kiowas who wiped out Elliott, Little Beaver," growled Pryor. "Reckon they come over to help Black Kettle, but lost their nerve when they seen how many soldiers Custer has."

Satanta braced his body, fighting as best he could. The Kid struck him a crack over the head with his gun barrel to quiet him. Limp, Satanta was slung on the dun's back, head hanging on one side, feet on the other, and was swiftly carried back toward the battlefield. It was not a long run, and they reached the spot ahead of the furious, pursuing braves, who dared not trail them in too closely.

It was ten o'clock in the morning, and the Battle of the Washita had been raging since four. The field was strewn with dead while wounded were being picked up. Firing was dying off. Only occasional explosions rang out as here and there a handful of warriors made a final stand, refusing to surrender.

Custer had won an important victory, skillfully using his eight hundred trained men and catching the enemy from all sides, cutting off escape. In this brilliant surprise blow he had smashed the terrible threat to southern Kansas. It was the greatest defeat ever administered to the Indians, to date.

Already the famous Indian fighter was taking full advantage of his triumph. Squads of dismounted cavalrymen were quickly setting fires to tepees and captured war equipment of the murderous hostiles. Great herds of Indian mustangs had been rounded up, to cripple the Indians if they contemplated further raids.

The Kid rode up to the busy general.

"I got Satanta, Gen'ral," he informed, "and there's a big bunch of Kiowas up on the hills! Fact, there's thousands of braves in the vicinity."

"Good work, Pryor," said the general, highly pleased at the capture the Rio Kid had made, for Satanta was one of the most troublesome Indian chiefs with whom the Army had to deal.

Bugles rang out, and squadrons of mounted troopers began forming.

"We'll hit those Kiowas fast, before they can collect themselves," General Custer said.

An ammunition train had broken through to the fighting troops. The wagons were not far away, and wounded must be transported. There was a welter of detail for staff officers to take care of, and prisoners had to be guarded and questioned.

The Kid made his report on the death of Major Elliott and his squadron. Sadly Custer shook his handsome head, with its flowing golden hair.

"We've lost good men today, Pryor," he said soberly. "Hamilton, Elliott — too many."

His brother Tom was wounded, not mortally, but painfully. He and other injured soldiers were being taken care of by Dr. Lippincott as fast as the trained surgeon could work.

Three hundred picked fighting men followed Custer and the Rio Kid along the winding bank of the Washita. They swept the beaten, disheartened Indians before them. All fight had gone out of the Cheyennes and their allies.

They found the Kiowa village deserted, and took large supplies that would prevent the Indians from making further raids. The Arapahoes were gone, and with what they could snatch up, the hostiles were heading rapidly westward for the wilds of Texas and Dakota.

The troopers were worn from the long night and the hard battle. Horses must rest, be cared for, the men had to be fed and allowed to sleep.

Having driven the enemy out of the district, allowing his wagon train to break through, General Custer returned to the Cheyenne village, where Black Kettle, the leading spirit of the Dog Soldiers, lay dead with many of his braves.

The Kid swung from the dun. He was covered with powder streaks and blood, from his wounds received in hand-to-hand encounters.

"Gen'ral," he suggested, "how about John Vandon, the Indian Agent? He armed Black Kettle and Satanta, egged 'em on to attack Kansas settlements. He's a friend of that Black Buffalo, who ain't captured yet. Vandon's busted all the laws the Government ever made, sellin' likker to the Indians, armin' hostiles. I reckon he could be arrested without much trouble, though he has a bunch of gunmen hangin' 'round his place."

Custer nodded.

"You're right, Pryor." The general's lips were grim. "Vandon also sent Keyes to kill you." He swung, looking over his officers. "Lieutenant Dixon!" he called.

Frank Dixon stepped up, saluting. The young lieutenant, who had fought bravely through the long battle, encouraging and leading his troop, had two slight wounds — an arrow scratch on one cheek and a bullet burn on his left hand.

"Lieutenant," ordered the general, "take twenty of your men, make sure they have ammunition and emergency rations, and accompany Pryor to the Vandon agency. He'll scout for you. Arrest Vandon and bring him to me. We expect to strike north for Camp Supply, but no doubt you'll reach there ahead of us."

Custer swung back on the sullen Satanta, who was awake, rubbing his head. Satanta's dark eyes fixed the general. Custer wished to question Satanta, but the chief only folded his arms, glaring at his captor, refusing to answer.

The Kid waited, smoking and resting, while Dixon got his troopers ready for the march. Wailing squaws and taciturn braves, prisoners from the big fight, were thick as ants in the humming ruins of Black Kettle's great village.

Custer was in a hurry, and he made that fact known.

"We must get out of here before they have a chance to collect themselves," he ordered.

As they had drawn back to the battlefield, large numbers of mounted Indians — Kiowas, escaped Cheyennes, Arapahoes, Apaches and others — had trailed in, but remained at a respectful distance, watching the actions of the troops.

They showed no disposition to fight, but as Custer started his advance guard off, melted away.

Still the soldiers were aware that they were not yet out of danger. If the chiefs could rally their braves, the victory might turn into a massacre after all.

Chapter XXI
Indian Agent

Failing to find Sue Miller in the Cheyenne village had hit Lieutenant Dixon hard, but he was a soldier, and the hard fighting had helped him to steel himself against the bitter disappointment.

He was glad to be busy, and quickly saw to his picked squadron which was to accompany the Rio Kid and help in John Vandon's arrest. Cartridge boxes were filled, rations issued, horses seen to.

"All ready, Kid," he reported presently.

The Kid swung to the dun, and Celestino Mireles, mounted on a fresh horse that his expert eye had picked from the Indian mustangs, fell into line. Dixon and Bob Pryor rode together at the front of the squadron, with Mireles following close. A few paces behind, came Sergeant Oley Olsen and his men.

"Do you think we'll ever find her?" inquired Dixon, as they swiftly left the humming battlefield behind them, heading along the Washita toward the agency.

He watched the Kid's grim face, drawn up by the Stetson chin-strap, for a ray of hope.

"I didn't see any sign of her in the other villages," replied Pryor.

Dixon knew his friend meant to urge him to keep up hope.

"They could easily have run her into the hills or killed her and left her in the forests," he said. "I can face it, Kid. The Frontier has taught me something. Anyhow I'm glad we found Ollie."

For a time they rode on, their horses' hoofs crunching the snow which had settled under sun and wind.

"Mebbe Custer'll get information out of Satanta and the other prisoners," the Kid suggested, but Dixon shook his head.

"I've learned a bit about Indians, too," he said glumly. "They're awful liars. They won't dare tell the truth about her. They'd be afraid of punishment."

The Rio Kid shrugged. On the Frontier and the wild trails he had grown used to looking the Grim Reaper straight in the eye and smiling. Most pioneers had to face harsh facts and could not permit tragedies to overwhelm them. Life must go on, no matter what happened to loved ones in a dangerous land.

They rode through the afternoon, and took an hour's rest near sundown. Then the Kid, knowing the direction they must take to reach Vandon's agency on the Cimarron, left the valley of the Washita and cut across country toward the post.

Riding the snowy trail, with his coat collar up against the biting night wind, Dixon thought this new-found scout friend of his must be made of steel and hickory, for the Kid was never tired.

The moonlight was bright, the stars twinkling in the frosty November air, the bleak shadows of the bare tree limbs striking the gleaming snow. The leather of the troopers behind creaked, and now and then metal accoutrements jangled as the men half-dozed in their saddles, hypnotized by the steady pace set by the scout.

It was an hour past midnight by the moon when the Kid suddenly drew up.

"There it is," he said.

The agency was spread before them, down the slope on the banks of the Cimarron. It was dark, save for fires still glowing in the reservation Indians' camp across the river.

"I'll go in first and check up, Dixon," the Kid said. "Place yore men in a circle round the house. Careful they don't shoot any innocent folks who come runnin' out. Vandon's men sleep in the house."

Dismounting in the concealing shadows of the timber, they checked their weapons, and the Kid stole, a swift ghost, toward Vandon's log home. Dixon and Sergeant Olsen gave their orders in low voices, and the troopers, on foot, swiftly formed a circular line, closing in on Vandon's.

The Kid came stealing back to Dixon, signaled him.

"All sound asleep," he whispered. "We'll go in the back way. Olsen and Celestino can hold the front under their guns."

Pistol in hand, Dixon followed the Kid to the rear door of John Vandon's house. No sounds could be heard from within. Presently the Kid tried the latch. The door was locked.

"Push it in," Dixon said.

He put his stalwart shoulder to the panel, and the Kid shoved with him. The bolt tore from its crude fastenings and they jumped into the darkness of the kitchen.

As they paused in the middle of the floor, trying to accustom their eyes to the blackness, a gruff voice called from another room:

"Who's that?" And they heard the *cluck-cluck* of a gun being cocked.

"Vandon!" breathed Pryor. "C'mon."

They crept forward silently.

"Yuh red rascals, if yuh try to steal any more sugar I'll put a load of buckshot into yore hides!" a man bawled almost in their ears.

Evidently John Vandon, the burly agent, believed he had to deal with thieving Indians.

"Down!" the Kid cried suddenly, and Dixon felt a strong hand pulling at his shoulder.

As they ducked, a shotgun roared. They saw the yellow flash of exploding powder, and scattering buckshot rained on the wall over them.

In the instantaneous light, they saw Vandon, his shaggy black hair sticking out from his massive head and his black beard bristling. They caught the gleam in his small, greenish eyes, still heavy with sleep, for he had been asleep when the crashing of the door had roused him.

"Throw down that gun, Vandon!" Dixon sang out. "You're under arrest."

But the Kid did not take such a chance. He knew the agent too well, and counted on having to hold off at least a dozen of Vandon's gunmen before the troopers could run inside.

His pistol snapped at the shotgun's flash, and the big agent cursed. The wall shook, and Dixon heard a heavy body thud against the floor.

"Strike a light," the Kid ordered, springing forward, gun in hand.

Dixon lit a match, sighted a candle on the board table, and touched his light to it. In its yellow illumination, he saw the Kid bending over the fallen Indian agent, removing the shotgun from his big hands.

"He ain't hurt much. . . . Careful now, Dixon! He's got plenty of helpers. Call yore men in."

Still there was no general alarm. Sergeant Olsen hurried inside, with half a dozen troopers.

Lieutenant Dixon ranged through the house, searching every room. When he returned to the kitchen he found the Kid squatted beside the unconscious Vandon, staring at a paper.

"Found this in Vandon's pocket, Dixon," Pryor said. "Read it."

The lieutenant scanned the white sheet. It read:

Send me as many men as you can, at once. Have them bring six cans blasting powder and meet me in the timber south of Lee's fort. Custer's gone to clean up the Indians and with the bulk of the settlers out of the way we can't lose.

Henderson

"Who's Henderson?" asked Dixon, puzzled. The Kid shrugged. "Dunno. I heard Vandon sing out his name once before. But it looks mighty bad for the folks at Lee's. Looks to me as though this Henderson skunk means to use that blastin' powder on the fort."

"I'd better send a report to Custer at once, then."

"And we ride for Lee's as fast as we can!"

A bucket of water with a thin coating of ice on it stood near. The Kid broke the ice and dashed the water into the giant agent's face, for he could see that his slug had only clipped Vandon's skull.

With a gasp and a yell, John Vandon returned to consciousness.

He struggled to rise, but the Kid, with a hard right, slapped him back against the wall.

"Who's Henderson, that wrote yuh this note, Vandon?" he demanded. "What's he mean to do with six cans of blastin' powder at Lee's fort? Why d'yuh want the Indians wiped out and the settlers killed?"

220

Vandon's eyes were round as green marbles. Despite his huge body and outward toughness, he feared the lithe Rio Kid. He took in the grim Dixon, the grizzled cavalry sergeant, and his troopers.

"I ain't talkin'," he muttered.

The Kid seized his throat, banged his head against the wall.

"Cut it out — stop," yelped Vandon, shielding his face with his arm.

"I'll tear yore heart out, Vandon!" snarled the Kid.

Intimidated by Bob Pryor, the Indian agent began to crack. He did not mean to tell everything, but as he let out one secret after another, the skillful prodding of the Rio Kid brought the full confession.

Lieutenant Dixon listened in amazement, appalled at the horrible crimes that Vandon admitted.

"We — we wanted the land between the railroad and the Antelopes. Yeah — yeah, we egged the Injuns on to hit the settlers so's we could step in and take their ranches and farms!"

"But why?" demanded Dixon.

"Talk, pronto," snarled Pryor, prodding Vandon with his boot toe.

"There's — a fortune in it. Railroad'll be built through there, shore, to the mines."

"I savvy." The hint was enough for the Kid. "What is it — gold?"

"Gold and silver, too. We — couldn't get it out with so many hostiles controllin' the Territory and south Kansas. 'Tain't my fault. Henderson, the boss, figgered it out, not me. He thought the soldier'd chase the Injuns west, and with most of the settlers dead, we'd win millions."

"Where are these mines?"

Vandon's lips pursed. Vaguely he waved westward.

"The Injuns brought us nuggets," he growled.

"I'll bet yuh mean the Antelope Hills!" cried the Kid. "California Joe and me seen plenty of shinin' metals up there!"

"Yuh devil!" snarled Vandon.

"This Henderson feller yuh call yore boss," prodded the Kid. "He sent for the blastin' powder to finish off the folks at Lee's fort?"

Vandon nodded.

"How long a start yore men got?"

"They rode off at sundown last night."

The Kid swung on Dixon.

"Get yore men mounted, pronto, Dixon. We got to overtake 'em if we can. I hope we make the fort in time."

The lieutenant called his orders to Ser-

222

geant Olsen. The military commands to horse, and mount rang out as Dixon hustled to the moonlight clearing of the agency. He left the Rio Kid bent over the infamous Vandon, dragging the big man's last secrets from him.

CHAPTER XXII
BLOOD ON THE SNOW

Miles out ahead of Dixon's squadron, the Rio Kid had outdistanced his partner, Celestino Mireles, in the race northwest for Lee's fort.

"We got to make it in time, Saber," he told his mount as, low over the dun, he kept his horse in the beaten track left by fifteen white gunfighters and as many renegade Indians sent to the mysterious boss, Henderson, by Vandon.

Dixon was coming behind with his men. The troopers were bringing John Vandon along, to hand him over to General Custer.

"Thank Heaven for this snow," muttered Pryor.

Because of it he did not have to leave his saddle to check up on the killers he was following, for in the snow the horse tracks were clear, even in the moonlight. The killers ahead had also been forced to break trail, which had slowed them somewhat, and now dawn was beginning to streak the sky.

What the Kid had pried out of John Vandon had made him see much more clearly the enormity of what Vandon's boss had done. It had not taken so much urging on Henderson's part to spur Black Kettle and Satanta to take to the war-path. Once started, they might have raided promiscuously, but Henderson had directed their fiendishness toward special targets, such as Miller's ranch, and whatever south Kansas settlements the boss, as Vandon called him, wanted out of his way.

This he had done ruthlessly, with the double purpose of bringing down the wrath of the Army on the Indians, and destroying the pioneers, in order to acquire their claims.

The light increased until the dun's hot breath was gray vapor in the frosty air. The Rio Kid broke from the woods and galloped across a clear space, with the little river, on which Lee's fort stood, a mile away. Already he could see the irregular lines of cottonwoods on the banks.

Turning west along the stream, skirting the brakes, he hunted a crossing.

"We oughtn't to be long now," he grunted, and then, over the farthest hill, he saw a column of smoke rising to the sky. "Lee's," he thought.

Turning Saber toward the creek, he slid down the clay bank, and splashed across the stony bottom, the icy water coming to his stirrups. The dun climbed the north bank to the plain, running full-tilt with the water streaming from his hide.

Eagerly the Kid strained forward. Did that smoke come from a cook fire, or had the fort been blown sky high?

Suddenly a bullet whistled close by his head, zipping through the bare trees and bushes. He drew a Colt, to shoot back, turning in his saddle.

"Stop that man!"

A bunch of men, clad like Indians, their faces smeared with dirt and paint, leaped on their horses and came charging across the creek to cut him off. He fired into them, to slow them, as he swung up the slanting slope toward the fort.

As he topped the crest of the last rise, with the howling, shooting gunmen coming after him, he sighted Lee's fort. A man was riding away from the place, low over a swift horse. The Kid snapped a revolver shot at him but the range was too long, and the dun was traveling at a mad pace.

Tearing toward Lee's, the Kid whooped a warning as he bore in. Sam Lee appeared, rifle in hand. Others, shoving behind him, stared at the approaching horseman.

"What's wrong?" cried Lee, catching at the Kid's stirrup as Pryor slid to a halt close to the gates.

"Get — everybody out — pronto!" gasped the Kid. "Yore fort's mined! It may go up any second!"

Shouts rose on the cold November air. Pryor ran into the fort with the others, starting the women and the children and late sleepers out.

They shooed the bewildered settlers ahead to a safe distance. Hardly had the last man hustled away from the fort than there came the roar of a terrific explosion. A second, a third, a fourth — and more — welded into one vast, terrible uproar that shattered the ear-drums and filled the air with flying debris and vast clouds of smoke.

Across the flats raced the great echoes, and the pioneers stared, white-faced, at the hole in the ground where they had been but a short time before, and where most of them would have perished had not the Rio Kid brought the warning. Stunned, it was minutes before they could realize that some murderous spy had mined their stronghold, had planned to kill them all.

Lee, teeth gritted, eyes dark with fury,

seized the Kid's arm.

"Who done it?" he demanded.

"Look around and see who's missin'," ordered Pryor. "Then get yore fightin' men ready, Lee."

"Let's see. . . . Why, nobody's missin', but that Dobbs feller that done rode out a few minutes ago!"

"Right the first time," the Kid told him coolly. "Edward Dobbs is a faker. His real name's Henderson and he's been pushin' Satanta and Black Kettle against yuh to take over yore land. He's been ridin' on their raids. C'mon, they ain't got much of a start."

Lee sang out orders. Grim-faced pioneers, every one a crack shot, swung into saddles. They started down to the river, crossing on the trail of the thirty renegades who had brought the blasting powder to Dobbs, and had stood by to help finish off any survivors of the explosions after he had planted the mines in the darkness before dawn. Lighting slow fuses, Henderson, alias Dobbs, had allowed himself time to get away from the fort. In those minutes, the Kid had been able to save the settlers.

Swift on the track of the killers, and with the trail easy to follow in the snow, the Kid led the avengers. They rode up the slope out of the valley, and on the crest saw the retreating gang.

"Black Buffalo!" the Kid muttered.

Sam Lee spurred up beside him.

"I don't see Dobbs," Lee growled.

"He rides as Black Buffalo," the Kid snapped. "That's him, up in front. He posed as a missionary teacher to fool anybody who come to Vandon's agency. Then he fixed up as an Indian and rode with Satanta and Black Kettle. He wormed a secret about a gold mine out of 'em — the chief reason he wanted yore land."

"But he was wounded," Lee said, puzzled. "He was crawlin' when they found him and brung him to the fort."

"Shore. He took a slug in the fight that Joe, Mireles and I was in at Miller's ranch that day. He was bad hurt and figgered he could get help at yore place. He cleaned off his make-up, let his hoss go, then crawled to where the sentry seen him, and told yuh a whoppin' story. He was a white man, and yuh took care of him. Soon as he got strong enough, he sent word to Vandon and tried to finish yuh all off. . . . C'mon, ride! No time to talk!"

Slowly they were overtaking the thirty killers ahead. In range, the Kid began shooting, and Henderson, alias Black Buffalo, alias Edward Dobbs, returned the fire. His men, turning in their saddles, also let go. The air was filled with missiles.

Ahead, the dip once more rose in the wavy formation characteristic of the land. The snowy trail cut through a ridge with stunted trees and bare brush sticking up black against the white background.

A grin touched the Kid's wide lips. Far ahead, the sunlight had caught the brilliant surface of metal. Scintillating flashes in the sky told the Kid that Dixon and his squadron were coming in fast on the beaten trail, straight toward Dobbs' gang.

The man who was now disguised as Black Buffalo was hanging back, fighting fiercely, pistol flaming to slow the pursuers. The van of his men ran into the cavalry at the narrowest part of the gap, recoiled in terror as they found the way blocked by stalwart, well armed troopers.

Shouts of consternation rang out. Sliding to a halt in the snow, they sought to escape, breaking in all directions.

"Grab 'em, Dixon, grab 'em!" bellowed the Kid, his voice ringing across the white wastes.

Dixon realized the situation. He barked orders and his men yanked their service revolvers and began riding down the murderers, red and white. Swiftly the settlers closed in, and there was no escape.

Henderson, at the rear of the procession, jerked his rein hard. He swung off the beaten track, spurring his powerful black horse through the snow, seeking a way up the valley.

Shots followed him but he drove on. The Kid swerved, and cut after him. The dun kicked the settled snow up as his swift hoofs slugged a way, now and then sliding on a slippery bit of ground, or sinking into a snow-covered depression.

The Kid let go with his pistol, and evidently it whined too close for comfort for the masquerading Black Buffalo. He turned and the Kid could see the smeared face, the fierce sheen of the killer's eyes as he took aim and fired.

Low over Saber, Pryor urged his mount on. The second slug from Henderson's gun bit a chunk from the crown of the Kid's Stetson.

"The jig's up, Henderson!" he roared. "Vandon's told everything! Throw down and quit!"

Inexorably he was drawing up on his man. But Henderson knew what awaited him if he surrendered. Hate flamed in his eyes, his teeth gritted as he found that the dun was drawing up on his own magnificent black.

They tore up the hill, skirting great bare rock outcroppings and timber. The dun's powerful muscles strained with the supreme effort he was making to take his rider within fair shooting range of the quarry ahead.

Henderson looked around again. The Kid was almost upon him. He raised his heavy revolver. "Curse your hide, Rio Kid!" he shrieked.

His gun went off, but a second too late. Within twenty yards, the Rio Kid's thumb rose off the hammer of his gun. The bullet sped for its target, to lodge unerringly in Henderson's brain. Henderson's revolver blared, but the slug buried itself in the snow. The black horse slowed, swerved. Henderson slid from his leather and thudded in the snow.

The Kid, pistol ready, leaped from his saddle. Colt on his foe, he checked up. But Henderson, alias Dobbs, alias Black Buffalo, was dead.

Over the virgin whiteness of the snow a bright red spot was slowly widening.

Chapter XXIII
Little Beaver's Party

When the Rio Kid rode into Camp Supply, two days later, he led a spare horse behind him. Across the animal hung the stiffened corpse of Henderson, the man who had ridden as Black Buffalo, and, to deceive honest people at the agency, had posed as a British missionary, Edward Dobbs.

Some miles in his rear came Lieutenant Frank Dixon and his men, with the prisoners they had taken.

General George Armstrong Custer, with his wounded brother Tom and a squadron of fast riding troopers, had just reached the camp on the creek. They had also brought with them a captive — the Kiowa chief, Satanta.

General Phil Sheridan was greeting Custer, shaking his hand, smiling broadly.

"The most satisfactory battle ever waged against Indians!" Sheridan cried.

"Howdy, Kid!" a voice called. "What did

you pick up in the woods?"

That was California Joe, who had come along with Custer.

"Oh, hello, Joe!" The Kid motioned to the led horse. "Why say, that's Black Buffalo. But he was a white man, danged if he wasn't! Remember that mealy-mouthed missionary at Vandon's agency? Edward Dobbs? This is him — and also Black Buffalo, and another hombre. That day we rode up to Vandon's, there was an Army wagon train in and Dobbs was puttin' on his act. His real name is Henderson. Vandon spilled all the beans to me."

Little Beaver, the Osage chief, who had distinguished himself as a scout in the campaign, stared at the dead man.

"Good scalp," he grunted. "Me savvy him, Kid. Him ride 'long Sa-tan-ta an' Mo-ke-ta-va-ta."

Satanta watched disdainfully, arms folded, his dark face never changing expression.

"Here's yore pard, Black Buffalo, Satanta," growled the Kid. "Yuh see what happened to him?"

Satanta grunted, shrugged, and turned away. Custer came over to shake hands with the Kid and ask about the dead man Pryor had brought in. In swift words the Kid explained the game played by Henderson.

"Real name's 'Butch' Henderson, Gen'ral. He's a killer from the East."

"Gold and silver in the Antelopes!" exclaimed Custer.

"Yeah. Ask Joe." The Kid smiled at his old friend.

"Huh, me?" California Joe asked innocently.

"No use to try to fool us, Joe," the Rio Kid declared. "I seen yuh sneakin' along the creek that day we scouted for the ford. Yuh was huntin' gold."

Joe blinked. He seemed flustered. He fixed his eyes on the Rio Kid.

"Why, doggone yuh, Kid, if I didn't know yuh so well I'd say yuh was in earnest! Yuh got the laugh on me. Why rub it in?"

"What yuh mean?" It was the Kid's turn to be puzzled.

California Joe slapped his padded knee. "Well, yuh do believe it! Thought yuh was raggin' me all the time, Kid."

"How so, Joe?" demanded Custer.

"Why, that stuff in the Antelopes ain't worth nothin'," answered Joe. "It fooled me at first sight, and it might fool others who ain't as knowin' as I am. I been prospectin' forty years and I've got where I can tell Fool's Gold from the real thing when I look close enough. Ain't nothin' but pyrites and galena in them Antelope Hills."

"Then Henderson did it all for useless metal!" cried the Kid, staring at the dead face of his arch-enemy. He swung to Satanta. "Hear that, Chief? How about it? Black Buffalo was after gold."

"Black Buffalo want gold, all time gold," the Kiowa leader grunted. "Kiowa and Cheyenne have no gold. Sioux have gold, way off, many suns ride." He swept his arm majestically westward. "Black Buffalo love gold. Heap help Injuns. Da-ko-tahs trade gold to Kiowa and Cheyenne."

"Reckon I savvy," the Kid told Custer. "Black Kettle and Satanta could get the guns and stuff they wanted out of Dobbs, or Henderson, by givin' him gold. It come from the Sioux country, but they let him believe it come from the Antelopes, and he got fooled by that stuff there, thinkin' that was from their mine. The Indians are right crafty and they wouldn't say out-and-out where they got the treasure. Sooner or later, Henderson would've traced it to the Sioux, but he helped smash south Kansas 'cause he thought the gold was in the Antelopes."

A rest and a hot meal did wonders for the Rio Kid. Frank Dixon and his squadron rode in to report, fetching the prisoners they had taken. John Vandon, broken by the Kid,

236

confessed to Custer. Henderson, he repeated was a criminal from the East who had had a hold upon him — enough to blackmail him and make him follow orders.

The Kid knew that the main campaign in south Kansas and the Indian Nation was coming to its climax. The Seventh would go into camp to the north. Over his heart hung a dark pall, however. There could be no real triumph in what he had so far helped to accomplish until he was certain Sue Miller was dead. The thought of her a captive, beaten by squaws and braves in some far-off Indian village, tortured him.

Lounging in his tent with Celestino Mireles stretched near him, he grew aware of two black, beady eyes watching him from the flap.

"Why, howdy, Little Beaver," he sang out. "Come in."

Little Beaver's dark face, with its flat, broad nose and long jowls, was stolid and expressionless as he sat outside, staring in. Like most Indians, he hid his emotions behind a mask.

At the Kid's invitation, the tall chief came in. He wore deerskin-fringed leggings, a hide jacket, feathers in his black hair, and was painted with victory colors. His people had been massacred by the stronger tribes,

Kiowas and Cheyennes, cut down to a fraction of what they had once been, and Little Beaver and his Osages had only been taking their revenge when they had scouted for and fought with the white man. Scalps hung at Little Beaver's belt, where rode his long knife and tomahawk and pistols, for he still was a savage.

"Heap big scout," he grunted gutturally, touching the Rio Kid's arm.

He was voicing his admiration for the Kid's fighting prowess. Friend or enemy, it was this which counted most with an Indian. Always the laurels were to the strong, to the winner.

"Yuh're a fine warrior yoreself, Little Beaver," complimented the Rio Kid.

"Little Beaver go back to tepee. You come. Dance. Good squaws."

The Kid grinned. "He's invitin' us to a party, Celestino. What say we go?"

"*Si,* General," agreed Mireles. "What you say."

Thirty hours later, Little Beaver and his Osages, honorably discharged and paid off by General Custer, led the way into the Osage village. It was many miles south of the Kansas line, in the Indian Nation, but cunningly concealed and out of the way of the marauding Dog Soldiers.

When the Kid and Mireles arrived with Little Beaver, they saw some three dozen tepees stood on the banks of a small brook, in the thick woods.

Whoops of triumph rang out as the squaws and those who had been left behind greeted their chiefs. Scalps were displayed, those scalps taken by Little Beaver and his scouts in the Washita battle and on the trail.

The Kid swung off the dun. Little Beaver proudly led him to his tepee. They were waited on, hand and foot, by squaws, plied with delicacies.

After a time one of the Osage chief's followers entered and spoke for a time with Little Beaver in their own tongue which the Kid did not understand. Little Beaver showed as much excitement as any Indian ever does. He turned to the Kid, rose, and ordered: "Come!"

Puzzled, the Kid trailed the chief and his braves to a large tepee, heated by a fire inside and well lined with buffalo robes. In the shadowed light he saw a figure lying, warmly covered with furs, and with a squaw kneeling beside it.

"Sick?" asked the Kid.

"See," Little Beaver replied.

The chief pulled back the covering from the face, and the Kid almost leaped out of his boots.

"Sue! Sue Miller!"

The girl gazed up into his face.

"I — I know you!" she whispered.

The Kid seized her hand.

"Yuh all right? They ain't hurt yuh?"

"No. The Indians have been very kind. But my leg is broken."

The astounded Kid plied her with questions.

When the terrible attack had started on the ranch, Sue said, she had run out, mounted a horse and ridden for the Lee's to fetch help. A bullet had hit her and in her agony she had lost her way, although her horse had kept on running and had eluded the attackers in the darkness.

She had been able to cling to consciousness but unable to guide the horse, had hung on, terrified, instinct causing her grip to remain tight.

"I don't know how long I rode," she said. "Finally I did lose my senses, and when I woke up I was being carried on a horse in front of an Indian. I thought the Cheyennes had me. They kept on and on and finally brought me here."

"Injun find in woods, heap near dead," explained Little Beaver. "No hurt. Osage friend of paleface."

"Yuh've done fine, Little Beaver," the Kid cried enthusiastically.

He gave orders to Mireles, and the Mexican rode for Camp Supply.

Sue was still weak and in pain. The bullet had splintered her shin, the Kid found, but luckily the big leg bone had kept the limb straight.

"It ain't bad, Sue," he encouraged. "A surgeon'll soon fix yuh up. I'm mighty glad to see yuh. And Frank Dixon'll be plumb happy. He's eatin' his heart out over yuh."

Her eyes sparkled. She could still smile. Then her face became drawn, anxious, once more.

"Father — and Mother?" she whispered.

"I hate to tell yuh, but yuh must know. They're — dead, Sue. But Andy and the two little boys are safe and sound. . . ."

Three days later, Lieutenant Dixon, Andy Miller, and several troopers arrived at Little Beaver's village. With them came an Army surgeon to tend the injured girl.

"Ambulance is on the way, Kid," Sergeant Olsen reported.

The Kid slouched in the tepee door. Andy Miller had kissed his sister, overjoyed at sight of her, unharmed save for the leg wound.

"She'll soon be all right," the doctor

241

reported. "When the ambulance comes, she can be taken home."

"Home?" repeated Andy Miller. "It's burnt to the ground."

"We can build it again," Sue said.

She was looking now, not at her brother, but at Lieutenant Dixon, who knelt at her side.

The Kid watched the two for a moment, happy at finding each other after such cruel separation.

"I reckon Kansas'll be all right," he murmured.

As for the Rio Kid, settling was not in his line. The wild ways called his restless nature, the wilderness trails of the Frontier, covered by the swift hoofs of the battle-loving dun.

ABOUT THE AUTHOR

Tom Curry was born in Hartford, Connecticut and graduated from college with a degree in chemical engineering. Leo Margulies, editorial director for N. L. Pines's Standard Magazines, encouraged Tom to write Western stories. In 1936, Margulies launched a new magazine titled *Texas Rangers*. Leslie Scott wrote the first several of these 45,000-word novelettes about Texas Ranger Jim Hatfield, known as the Lone Wolf, published under the house name Jackson Cole. Tom Curry's first Jim Hatfield story was "Death Rides the Rio" in *Texas Rangers* (3/37) and over the succeeding years he contributed over fifty Hatfield tales to this magazine alone. Curry also wrote three of the series novelettes for *Masked Rider Western* and some for *Range Riders Western*. It was in 1938 that Margulies asked Curry to devise a new Western hero for a pulp magazine and Tom came up with Bob Pryor. *The Rio Kid Western* published its first issue in October 1939. Subsequently Curry expanded several of his Rio Kid stories to form novels, published by Arcadia House, with the hero's name changed from Bob Pryor to Captain Mesquite. Possibly Curry's best Western fiction came during the decade of the 1940s, especially in the Jim Hatfield stories and in his Rio Kid novelettes. After Margulies was released from Standard Magazines, Curry quit writing and began a new career in 1951 with Door-Oliver, Inc., that lasted for fourteen years, working in their research and testing laboratory in Westport as accountant, purchasing agent, and customer service representative, making use at last of his chemical engineering degree. When Curry retired from Door-Oliver, he resumed writing Westerns sporadically for Tower Books and Pyramid Books and, later still, for Leisure Books. In October 1969, Margulies informed Curry that he was to be publishing a new digest-sized publication to be titled *Zane Grey Western Magazine* and he wanted Tom to write some new stories to appear in its pages featuring a number of Zane Grey's best known characters. These stories would be published under the house name Romer

Zane Grey. Curry put a lot of talent and energy into so many of his Western novelettes, particularly the Rio Kid adventures, and his stories can still intrigue and entertain.